To Richard, Mowt and Geoff,
who are not represented,
even heavily disguised,
in this book

ALL THE
MATERIALS
FOR A
MIDNIGHT FEAST

or

Zagira

Old Street Publishing Ltd
Trebinshun House, Brecon LD3 7PX
www.oldstreetpublishing.co.uk

ISBN 978-1-908699-18-3

10 9 8 7 6 5 4 3 2 1

A CIP catalogue record for this title is available from the British Library.

Typeset by Old Street Publishing Ltd.

Printed and bound in Great Britain.

ALL THE MATERIALS FOR A MIDIGHT FEAST

or
Zagira

GARY DEXTER

OLD STREET PUBLISHING

Swift was then about forty-seven, at an age when vanity is strongly excited by the amorous attention of a young woman.

– Samuel Johnson, *Lives of the Poets*

Walk by my side in the garden
Turn off the road; it's there
For those who wish to find it.
Walk with me in the cool of the evening
Marvelling at the beauty of the garden
And the scents of its flowers.

– Anon, Chinese, 11th Cent.

PART ONE

Saturday 23rd October, 2010.
Hull Bus Station.
About 3.30 pm.

GUY'S VOICE is extraordinary. Tender, soft, low... When she phoned this morning I was quite taken aback.

'Nicholas,' she murmured, 'I'm organizing a coach to Glasgow today, and I still have some seats left. Would you like to come? It'd be really nice if you could.'

What a voice! I felt almost like a baby having its toes tickled. At the same time I was conscious of being quite shamelessly manipulated.

'If I could put you down,' Guy continued, 'that would be really great, because we must pay for this coach.'

'Oh all right, Guy,' I said.

'Thank you, Nicholas,' she said, and rang off.

Guy's full name is Gaia, but her friends call her Guy. Her last name is de Courcey, which means she has the sort of name found only in books about knights – Guy de Courcey. Her mother is Mrs de Courcey, the Liberal Democrat councillor.

Of course her extraordinary voice – like warm honey – is only deployed on certain occasions. On other occasions she can be quite curt, even rude. I met her in the street a couple of weeks ago and she cut me dead, as if I wasn't even there. She walked right past me, arm-in-arm with some girl. I'm sure she must have seen me.

Still – I didn't say hello to her either. So perhaps she thought *I* was snubbing *her*. Who knows what was going through her mind? What do the French say? *Tout comprendre c'est tout pardonner?*

And so here I am on this coach to the submarine base.

·

It is a dispiriting thing to fall in love during an epoch that is certain to see the end of the world.

Perhaps I should explain.

I was born on the 24th of October 1962, at the height of the Cuban Missile Crisis. It was a Saturday. It was on that Saturday, in fact, that Robert McNamara, the United States Secretary of State for Defence, left his home in the suburbs of Washington, DC, for his office in the Pentagon, and, as he kissed his wife and children goodbye, wondered if he would ever see them again. At that very moment, as Robert McNamara was kissing his wife, my mother went into labour. If this seems fanciful, I assure you it is not. I have looked into his autobiography and checked the time, and of course I have the testimony of my mother. I have worked it out to the hour, accounting for the time difference.

My arrival, then, was not merely during the Cuban Missile Crisis, but at its very apogee, at the point when the world looked most as if it were going to blow itself up. My mother told me, many years later, that thoughts of the end of the world had been drifting through her mind even as she was giving birth to me. What sort of a world was this to bring a child into? What was the use of going through all this pain and suffering? What was the point of it all?

Is there not at least a possibility that those thoughts were transferred to me in that terrible moment of nativity?

My early years were spent in the most unrelieved gloom.

I remember one incident that took place shortly after I left school. I was, by then, much haunted by a sense of impending catastrophe and was beginning to wonder how people could just go about their business as if nothing was happening. My mother and father were quite extraordinarily bluff and jovial, and appeared to be enjoying life, my mother having shed any real doubts about the future of the world when the radio ceased reporting its imminent destruction.

I was in the public library reading a newspaper. I was, I suppose, about sixteen years old, and it had not yet been decided whether I would take my A Levels and go to university. This was during the late 1970s, and the cold war was in a particularly nasty phase.

It was very quiet in the library, and there was a smell of floor polish. As I flicked through the newspaper, I came across an article. An early-warning siren had been installed on the village green of Inwardleigh, not very far from where we lived. A nice little village, with a duck-pond. Unfortunately I don't remember the headline – it must have been something like: 'Mayor Unveils New Siren'. But this wasn't what caught my eye. It was the first sentence of the article. I remember that first sentence with crystal clarity. It read as follows:

'Nuclear war will not go unnoticed in Inwardleigh.'

I remember reading this and being gripped by a fury I have rarely experienced before or since. I felt literally possessed. I rose from my chair with the newspaper in my hand, my scalp boiling.

'IDIOTS!' I shouted at the top of my voice.

The old man at the table across from me, who had been furtively eating a sandwich, stopped, his mouth hanging open. Inside was something unpleasant.

'IDIOTS!' I screamed once more, taking the newspaper and hysterically crumpling and ripping it up. My voice, and the ripping newspaper, were very,

very loud in the quiet of the library: everyone, from the oldest librarian to the tiniest child, were, I imagine, startled out of their wits. But I didn't care in the least. I felt that they all had it coming to them. I felt full of a godlike rage as I flung the remains of the paper away from me, not caring who or what I hit, and walked to the door, unfortunately leaving my coat behind on the back of the chair. I had still not yet said anything beyond that one repeated word, 'IDIOTS!', but as I got to the little counter with its glass partition, I realised what it was that I wanted to say. I turned to address the whole library, and, with great profundity of conviction, and not without a malicious glee, spacing my words carefully and precisely, announced:

'YOU – ARE – ALL – GOING – TO DIE!'

And with that I walked out.

This was very bad behaviour, girls, but I was very young.

•

I did, as it happened, go to university: to Hull University. I hope that you too will attend university. Unfortunately I left the university itself during the first term, and did not, in the end, get a degree in oriental languages as I had planned. My studies were curtailed due to illness.

However, instead of leaving Hull immediately and returning home to Bournemouth, I stayed on in student digs with some friends of mine, most of whom had similarly dropped out for one reason or another.

This is not a course of action I would now advise taking, unless it is for some very good reason.

THE COACH has just stopped and a very handsome young man has just got on. I vaguely recognize him, though I have never spoken to him. He calls himself 'Beaver'. Why any young man should be called – or call himself – 'Beaver', is a little perplexing.

Whatever the reason, 'Beaver' is something of a character. He is tall and burly, has a small beard, and is wearing camouflage trousers. He is one of those persons who, despite not being of Black or African origin, has managed to grow dreadlocks. It must have taken great effort to persuade his fine hair to assume those shapes. Some of the shapes, however, do not look much like dreadlocks. They look more like knots. His hair is very fair and silky, and many months or years of assiduous non-combing has allowed it to grow freakish knots, almost like eggs. I am reminded of the king rat, or rat-king, that forms when several rats are confined in some deep and smelly place from which they cannot, or do not wish to, escape. Their tails combine together – get knotted up – and they have to move as a single entity. I believe the largest king rat or rat-king ever discovered was composed of some forty rats – in Holland, I think.

But this isn't the most remarkable thing about 'Beaver'. The most remarkable thing, to my mind, is the camouflage fatigues I have already mentioned. This young man is an anti-nuclear protester. He is not a soldier. In fact, at our destination he may well find himself in confrontation with soldiers. Or policemen, at any rate. So the trousers seem to me to be utterly incomprehensible. Why on earth is he wearing camouflage fatigues? Does he feel that the trousers signify 'rebellion' against society's norms (despite the fact that the army is surely the most normative of all society's institutions…)? It is impossible to say. It is impossible to imagine asking him.

Another thing that makes the trousers remarkable, to my mind, is that the coach is full of young women. They are all eighteen, nineteen or twenty years old, mostly from the university. And these young women seem to have very little to say about his trousers. They seem very friendly with him… though perhaps they are only friendly on the surface, and underneath they despise him. Is that likely? After all, we are all bound on the same endeavour, striving for the same goal… If they don't see the trousers as an existential problem, or a problem in logic, or ethics, or, more to the point, politics, then why should I?

As above.

WELL, YOU probably want to know what this is about.

You know me for who I am now, a funny daddy with a tickly chin, a daddy whose job has something to do with Chinese people. I hope you too will have my interest in China when you grow up. Katy dear – you seem at the moment to be the one most interested in the Institute, but then you are the elder.

Your daddy, however, was not always what he is now, and that, I suppose, is what I'm trying to get at. I want to tell you a bit about myself as I was when I was younger. Some of my behaviour – such as what I'm doing today, on this coach – will doubtless seem a bit strange to you.

Perhaps I should continue where I left off, that is, at Hull. My memories of that time are now a little hazy – it was over a quarter of a century ago – but I remember a few things very clearly. For instance, the house.

It was a terraced property on Christiania Street, near the centre of town. The house was on three floors, and always seemed very cold and dark. I suspect that some of the bulbs had blown out and nobody had bothered to replace them. Only the individual rooms were ever heated, so that the communal areas were always freezing. There were clouds of little black flies in the kitchen in summer. It was, by our present standards, rather basic. (I think you will agree that our present house is nice and warm, and always clean and bright.)

The house was shared between five of us: three young men and two young women.

Soon after I first moved in I decided to decorate the house, and so I painted my room, as well as the hallway, the dining room and the kitchen, with pictures of dinosaurs. I did this in consultation with the other tenants, of course. But one young woman – her name was Madeleine – was overlooked: she came very rarely out of her room at the front of the house, and had been missed, I suppose. One afternoon I discovered her standing stock still in front of a seven-foot-high iguanodon in the dining room. Her expression suggested that she didn't like it.

'Who did this?' she asked.

'I did,' I said.

She paused. It seemed she was having trouble saying what it was she didn't like about it.

'It's a bit sexist,' she said finally.

I was dumbfounded. However, I did see her point. The iguanodon was an expression of some perhaps not very feminine energy. The odd thing was that while I was painting it I had no idea in my mind whether the iguanodon was male or female. It could easily, I thought, have been a female iguanodon.

Strangely enough this was the girl I later fell in love with. This was the 1980s, you understand, and it was not a very easy time to fall in love, as I have already said. The problem was not simply the prospect of nuclear annihilation. In those days it was not considered polite to attempt to initiate any relationship between the sexes. Such a thing could easily be interpreted as an affront. That, at least, is how it seemed to me at the time. Of course, there are still some people who feel like that today. Guy, for instance.

At any rate, in the 1980s, certain things were not done and certain things were not spoken of. One of the things that was not done was approaching any young woman and slyly putting your arm around her, while very, very drunk; and I admit I was drunk or I never would have tried it.

This occurred some time after the iguanodon incident. Madeleine and I were in the kitchen, where I had been boiling mussels. Hull is a fishing town, of course, and seafood of all types is cheap and plentiful. Madeleine had just made it clear that she disapproved of what I was doing – that is, boiling the mussels – and in fact had gone so far as to accuse me of being a 'cannibal'; and it was at that point that I put my arm around her. She wriggled free from my grip, and I was too drunk, I suppose, to see that she was very displeased indeed. I laughed, and must have made some attempt to apologize, but the next thing I knew, a heavy boot – young women in the 1980s all wore boots, of the type more commonly seen today on fell-walkers – was heading on a trajectory straight for my groin. I should say to you, girls, that the groin is that part of a man's body between his legs, and it is very painful if kicked.

Now, it has been proven that the unconscious regulates nine-tenths of all human behaviour; and in this case my unconscious served me very well. Despite my being drunk, I managed to take a half-step back – I could not have gone much further back, because the cooker with its pot of boiling mussels was behind me – and my hands shot down to the area where the boot was scheduled to arrive. The result was that boot and hands met. I found myself, in fact, tightly clasping Madeleine's ankle. Madeleine had not made contact, as she had expected, with the region she had aimed for, and instead of the result she had pictured – that of me folding up and collapsing – found herself gripped tightly by one ankle.

We were both, as you may imagine, utterly shocked by the turn of events. I was shocked to be suddenly gripping her ankle, and she was shocked to be, instead of my vanquisher, my abject prisoner. Only fifteen seconds earlier, we had been talking about mussels. Madeleine was now hopping slightly on one leg to stay upright. At that moment I felt more than ever apologetic, but considered that it would be unwise to let the leg go just yet: she might wish to resume kicking.

I should mention at this point something I have omitted, though it is not really relevant – there were several other people in the room. One was Henry, a co-tenant, and the other was a young man whose name for the life of me I can't remember, the other male co-tenant; and there may have been some other girls, perhaps friends of Madeleine's. They were all watching with interest as events unfolded.

Madeleine didn't say anything, and instead simply regarded me with a look of disbelief, breathing heavily through her nostrils. Her ankle felt quite delicious, I will admit, even in that heavy boot. I felt I had almost a right to touch it, since she had so recently tried to deal me a blow in the groin with it – I felt a moral right to it, I might say. And so, feeling my moral right to its continued possession, I pushed Madeleine a little backwards, with the result that she was forced to hop backwards on one leg. This seemed to me highly amusing – which I can see now was reprehensible – but I was, as I have said, very drunk. I made her hop back, then to one side, then to the other, all the time without either of us uttering a word (that I remember) and then I'm afraid I shoved her down, like a heap of dirty washing, into the corner by the sink. She went down with a great thump in a heap of orange dress in the corner. I thought to myself: 'I'm in for it now' – I had made up my mind not to defend myself in any way, and was ready to submit to any kind of punishment – when Madeleine simply picked herself up and walked out of the kitchen door, and into the night. It was winter and she had no coat on.

As you might understand, I was rather glad to see her go. I was also rather astonished. That sudden exit, without a word, without looking at me, without any expression I could decipher. What was going through her mind? Impossible to say! One moment she was in the corner like a rag-doll, and the next she was gone, and Henry's laughter was echoing around the small kitchen smelling of mussels. I, however, had no desire to laugh. I was, I suppose, beginning to fall in love with her – if I had not already. Yes – I certainly had already fallen in love with her because otherwise I would never have attempted to put my arm around her waist.

•

Certain passages will need to be cut out of this diary as unsuitable for children. I will flag the passage above for possible deletion. It's difficult – in fact it's impossible – to know what age they will be when they read it. They might be fifty, or they might be fifteen – or, I suppose younger than fifteen. Or maybe we'll all go together, in which case no one will read it.

I think near Market Weighton. Unfortunately I haven't brought my watch — but about 5.45.

Now, I have said already that the 1980s were distinguished by the fear of nuclear war. That statement could equally apply to the 1970s, the 1960s and the 1950s — even, I suppose, the 1940s. But I am qualified only to speak of the 1980s.

In the 1980s there was none of the current concern, perfectly justified, for the future of the planet, due to the release of certain gases. Nor were we preoccupied with 'terror' wrought by agents of foreign powers. Instead we lived in a permanent state of terror brought about by our own governments. Everyone expected the whole globe of the earth to be destroyed, suddenly, perhaps while we were in our beds, and completely, irrevocably. We were all convinced, my friends and I, who were all young, that the destruction of our world, our friends and family, and all our loves, was more or less assured, and that if there were any survivors they would eke out their remaining lives in the most horrible of circumstances, injured, sick, poisoned, cold, hungry, grieving, so that 'the survivors would envy the dead,' as someone said. Yes… It was not very nice in that time to be alive, and to be young was worse. Imagine our own idea of our own future! There was simply none… We expected to die at any minute. If not today, then tomorrow; if not tomorrow, then next week.

I remember that a young woman of my acquaintance — a really very remarkable and beautiful young woman — once told me — this would have been in 1981, in the first few weeks of my university course — that the world would in fact end in October 1982, when all the planets would be in alignment. When I heard her words, I remember, I was filled with an unreasoning joy. If she were correct, and if nothing else happened in the meantime, then we had a whole year before the end of everything, at which time I would have reached the quite advanced age of twenty. This was much more than I felt I had a right to expect. The idea that I might get to the age of forty-seven, or even see the year 2000, let alone 2010, I would have thought quite ludicrous, and perhaps even undesirable. In any case, even if by some miracle I did survive, I would, I presumed, by the year 2000, be so utterly changed that I would have nothing to do with myself as I had been, as a teenager. I could not really muster any interest in that remote figure, my future self. After all, it was I, as a teenager, who was in present danger, not that future self: it was I who expected at any moment to be buried in a collapsed house, or have my skin flayed off by a blast wave, or be blinded by a sudden bright light, or have my bones ground into the pavement by falling masonry... yes... luckily for you girls, that worry is now a thing of the past.

•

I must just tell you a little about this young woman, the one who informed me about the alignment of the planets. Her name was Hannah, which to me even now remains a very melodious name. In Japanese it means 'nose'. She was only seventeen, but was already a talented artist and musician. Her remark about the alignment of the planets – which was made very early on a warm, dusty, aromatic July morning, as we walked together in Winterbank – will lead you to think, perhaps, that she was rather empty-headed. But she was nothing of the sort. She was a quite remarkably intelligent person, with a style of beauty so severe that it would have been… Well, let me say merely that I can't imagine what sort of man would have been able to find within himself the temerity to…

I think she felt something for me, however, because she once appeared in front of me wearing only her underwear.

This took place at her parents' house. Hannah's mother was my tutor at the university, a woman by the name of Dr Closer. Dr Closer always used to kiss me hello and goodbye, not on the cheek, but full on the lips.

On this occasion I was in Dr Closer's living-room, deep in conversation with Dr Closer – just the two of us – when all of a sudden Hannah sauntered into the room dressed only in her underclothing. She walked past us, towards the sofa, as if this were quite normal, and sat down. She then began reading a magazine. She had a very nice shape. Dr Closer seemed quite scandalized by her daughter's behaviour, and told her sharply to go upstairs and put something on: Hannah gave her mother a cool look, got to her feet, and went back up the stairs to her bedroom. She didn't come down again.

A little after Hannah had gone, I said goodbye to Dr Closer – receiving a kiss on the lips – and left the house. I pondered Hannah's behaviour as I walked home. I don't believe I came to any immediate conclusion that night. I realised that Hannah's appearance in a state of near-undress was some sort of communication to me personally – she knew I was downstairs, alone, with her mother – but, unfortunately, I could not decide what that communication consisted of. I inclined at the time – and in fact still do – towards the idea that she had been making some sort of statement of a primarily intellectual nature. This statement was obscure, but might have been something such as the following: 'You and I, Nicholas, are not man and woman, but repositories of a spark implanted in us by the One to whom we must return, and thus conventional propriety does not apply to us.'

•

Unfortunately the passage above will have to be considered for deletion, though, as I have suggested, there was nothing impure involved, at all: quite the opposite.

•

Guy – what was she doing with that girl?

As above.

FOR SOME reason the phenomenon of nakedness, or semi-nakedness – your father apologizes, girls – seemed to me, at the time, to have a theological or philosophical dimension. The encounter with Hannah Closer in her underwear was mirrored by another event at around the same time. I have mentioned Henry, our housemate at Hull, who was there that time when Madeleine and I danced around the kitchen. Henry was a short, stocky chap, quite good-looking, with curly fair hair, an ex-student of history, I believe. Well, he became quite drunk one evening – there was a party going on – and began holding forth to a small crowd of people in the little dining room with the iguanodon. Houses in the 1980s – I haven't been in any similar since – used to have a dining room of quite unimaginable smallness between the hallway and the kitchen at the back. I have no idea what the architect was up to designing a room that small. It was only a little larger than the size of a double bed – it would certainly have been impossible to have put a double bed in it without having to bounce on the bed to get to the kitchen. The iguanodon was very conspicuous in so small a room, which is another reason why Madeleine had objected to it, I think.

Anyway, Henry was in this tiny room, drunk, and he looked at us, and said in his pleasant Humberside accent: 'We are the last generation ever to exist on earth.'

Of course, I knew that, but had never formulated it to myself in quite that way. It put rather a shiver up my spine. Henry himself seemed calm as he delivered himself of this statement. And then, with equal calmness, he began taking off his shoes and socks. After he had done that, and was standing before us in bare feet, he divested himself of his trousers. And then, I am afraid to say, he removed his underwear. After standing like that for a time, he sat down and pulled his shirt over his head: it was almost as if he were preparing for bed, and it was all done in the utmost seriousness. He was now quite naked. The little crowd of people in the dining room had been watching him closely throughout the performance, and any females who wished to have done so could have run from the room, though none had. Henry's sitting posture conveyed an impression of modesty. There was no laughter, nor even any comment. I think we were all simply weighing his words.

Yes, the last generation. Our ancestors had crawled up out of the mud, developed limbs, fought, loved, died... all through the countless ages... and now, here we were, at the end. The last generation. And Henry and the rest of us, in the little dining room with the iguanodon, no bigger than a double bed, were members of it.

Putting it that way makes it sound as if we and Henry and the dining-room had some sort of significance, even if only as an ironic comment. But none of us, I believe, saw any significance. There was only the *fact*. The fact of our imminent deaths. And his phrase 'the last generation' contained within it something quite striking. Our deaths would be soon. We wouldn't be able even to reproduce ourselves before the catastrophe. There would be no time.

He was quite right, I believe, to think at that moment that we would be members of the last generation. Yes, girls, that's the way we all thought in those distant days.

I think Guy and that girl are lovers. But I'm sure that Guy recently had a boyfriend.

I don't really think it is very respectful, or even wise, to speculate about the personal lives of others. That's their business. However, one possibility is this: Guy might have been pretending that she and the girl were lovers, in order to make a point of some kind. This is quite possible. I think it is sometimes done. But if this is so, then one must ask — what point?

I am obviously failing to put myself into Guy's shoes. She obviously thought it was right to suggest they were lovers… though they were not lovers…

Was it her intention to confuse us, the public? Perhaps she wished to épater les bourgeois?

But no. No — surely not. Guy is nothing but open and honest. She has a very clear, frank expression. Guy values the truth above all things.

Perhaps the solution is to see her behaviour as symbolic. Perhaps Guy was trying to say that we must always live in the ideal, even though reality may fall short; or, to put it another way, it would have been ideal had she and the girl been lovers, and the fact that they were not lovers should not necessarily be allowed to…

Could this be correct?

As above.

A GREAT deal is coming back now. For instance, *apropos* of Henry, I remember that he had a relationship with a much older woman, in her mid forties, before coming to university. She used to write him long letters in spidery handwriting. Henry once allowed me to read one of them. She even visited him, once, in Hull. That was quite a shocking event.

I suppose that I, now, in relation to most of the girls on this coach, stand somewhat as this woman stood towards Henry. That is, I am old enough to be their father. It is really rather an astonishing thought. I have never really considered myself old. And yet here I am, with all these young women. Do they see me as old? When I look at my face in the mirror I don't see an old man. I still seem like a boy, at least to myself. My nose is still freckled like a bird's egg. I still have the same abundant sandy hair. The face is a little parched and shrunken, perhaps; the skin around the eyes and mouth betrays a wrinkle or two, and I have a few grey hairs, particularly at the temples. But generally speaking, I don't think I look my age. Men at my time of life tend to have put on a bit around the middle, and to have lost a bit of hair, whereas I am as slim now, I think, as I was when I was nineteen, and still have just as much on top.

Actually, something quite funny happened recently: I met a woman who I hadn't seen since we were both teenagers. She herself had changed a great deal in the intervening period. She had borne four children. When she saw me, her mouth dropped open. 'You haven't changed at all!' she cried.

Immediately afterwards she rather ruined the effect by adding: 'Mind you, you weren't much to begin with.'

•

Apparently Henry consummated his relationship with this woman on a train between Bucharest and Prague. Such a thing sounds utterly unlikely, I know – as if he had been reading too many spy novels and simply made it up – but it occurred while Henry was in Eastern Europe on a student visit. The woman was not herself a Romanian or Czechoslovak, but a teacher accompanying him on that visit. This lends the story a more believable aspect, I think.

•

Obviously stories about what so-and-so did on a train, etcetera, etcetera, are not suitable for this sort of diary. But I would like to say just a little more of what passed between Henry and the woman. The letter Henry showed me was rather sad. Following the incident on the train, the woman had descended into a state of some distress: she had given up her job, begun seeing a psychiatrist, and so on… The handwriting seemed to betray this distress. It looked quite insane, reminiscent not of words but of hair, tangled up beyond recall. Henry, after I handed the letter back to him, laughingly crumpled it up and threw it into the wastepaper basket. I was a little shocked, I think, by that. In general, Henry didn't seem to have much understanding or appreciation of women. Yet he never had any difficulty finding girlfriends. One wonders what they saw in him. If he didn't have strong feelings for any of the young women he became involved with, why bother in the first place? Why entangle their young lives with his own? Or their middle-aged lives, as in the case of the woman?

Things changed quite drastically for Henry when he himself fell in love. But I don't think this is quite the place to go into it: I might fit it in later. I really must get this diary back on track.

I AM aware that I have a tendency to digress a little, girls, but I think the general drift of this narrative is fairly clear. I went to university; I left university; I continued living in the shared house; my co-tenants were Henry, the other young man whose name I can't remember, Lara (who I haven't yet told you anything about) and Madeleine (who I was in love with). I have introduced you to Hannah and to Dr Closer. And I have given descriptions of Guy and such persons as 'Beaver', who exist, as it were, in the present tense. So everything is going smoothly.

I would like to say a word or two about Dr Closer. She is, I think, one of the most remarkable women I have ever met. When I knew her, her Chinese was fluent. She had a working knowledge of several other East Asian languages. She had written or edited a number of books on East Asian language, history and culture. All of this and she was still in her mid forties!

She was a remarkable-looking woman, too. She had a very striking face: all of her features were strong. Her forehead and chin were powerful. Her eyes were large, dark and deep. Her nose was big and a little irregular. Her mouth was full and wet, and her teeth were uneven.

But I know what you are thinking. No, no and no again! She was emphatically not ugly, nor even plain. In fact, she was extraordinarily beautiful. Soon after getting to know a person, it seems to me, the details of their appearance begin to be influenced by forces from within. If they have a weak or petty inside, the face becomes weak and petty. Even great beauty begins to dim. But if they have a great inside, the face takes on that greatness. Even the most unpromising features, lit from within in this way, become suffused with beauty and charm.

Of course this is all rather obvious.

Perhaps I should tell you a little anecdote to do with Dr Closer, just to illustrate the sort of person she was.

It was during a seminar in the first month of term. I suppose there were about ten of us there. We were in Dr Closer's study at the university, and we were discussing the origins of sinography, that is, the Chinese writing system. One of the students present, a young man by the name of Rod, who I knew vaguely, didn't seem to be paying much attention. I think he'd had rather a late night. He seemed to be doing nothing but fiddling with the pencil case on the arm of his chair. He was contributing nothing to the discussion.

It soon became apparent that Dr Closer had noticed this boy Rod's lack of attention, and I saw her look once or twice at his hand on the arm of the chair. I was busy making notes. And then, suddenly, in mid sentence, Dr Closer's face contorted with fury.

'STOP FIDDLING WITH THAT ******* PENCIL CASE!!!' she screamed at the top of her voice.

Rod turned white. I thought that he was going to faint. Up until that moment his mind had probably been quite empty; but now I could see that his entire being was jangling as if he'd been plunged into a freezing lake, or tossed into a volcano.

For several moments no one in the study could breathe.

Then, after giving Rod one last, lingering, venomous look, Dr Closer simply returned to the topic at hand. The origins of sinography. Everything went on as before.

In a few minutes we were all breathing normally. Our palpitations died away; we began listening and talking as if nothing had happened.

Rod, needless to say, was unable to join in. He had been killed, almost.

The seminar finished and we left.

Thinking about it, the most remarkable and shocking thing about this incident was the word Dr Closer used. It was a rude word, girls, a very rude word, and so I have not put it down here. At the time I couldn't quite believe my ears. A world-renowned scholar! And in fact, by the time its echoes had died away I was already wondering to myself whether I had really heard it at all. Had I simply imagined it?

At the same time, Dr Closer's use of this terrible and awful word, and the intensity of her rage, did not diminish by one jot my respect and love for her. In fact it raised her in my estimation. I hope, girls, that I don't seem to be condoning what she did or offering you a bad example. I certainly don't think swearing is funny. But it seemed to me – at the time, I mean – that Dr Closer had revealed something extraordinary about herself. She was capable, alongside all her other gifts, of surrendering herself utterly to passion.

•

I must just also record another incident related to Dr Closer. Again, it was at the university, this time at a lecture. There were about fifty or sixty students present, and we were listening to a co-presentation by Dr Closer and another authority on Chinese grammar, a visiting American professor by the name of Dr Conybeare. Dr Conybeare was an older man with a spade beard.

It soon became apparent that Dr Closer and Dr

Conybeare didn't get along very well. They were both standing at the front of the lecture hall behind identical lecterns, about ten feet apart, but were not making eye contact. Whenever they had to refer to one another's work or opinions they did so with icy politeness.

At some point towards the end of the presentation Dr Conybeare took a question from the floor on some hoary point of Chinese grammar. He launched into an explanation; and when he had finished, he glanced – one of his rare glances – at Dr Closer.

It was at this juncture that Dr Closer evidently decided to break ranks. Taking the glance as her cue to speak, she began to add to Dr Conybeare's account with new information. Then, gradually, she began to test some of its assumptions. Finally, she began to undermine it completely.

Dr Conybeare was too experienced a teacher to let this affect him. He nodded judiciously while Dr Closer was speaking. But I don't think anyone was deceived. We knew that these remarks of Dr Closer constituted an attack on Dr Conybeare – nothing less – and we knew that Dr Conybeare would be compelled to respond in some way, to defend his assessment.

After Dr Closer had finished speaking, it was Dr Conybeare's turn. He soon began to make up some of the lost ground. He wasn't doing too badly, in fact, when Dr Closer broke in, this time quite intemperately. She questioned him in a manner almost mocking. A new spirit had entered the lecture hall: a feminine rapacity that would not be brooked. All of us sensed it. Dr Closer intended to give no quarter.

Dr Conybeare began to answer. But Dr Closer interrupted again. 'That can't really be the case,' she was saying. 'The foremost' – she paused – '*criterion* must be the relation of topic to object.'

As soon as I heard Dr Closer pronounce the word 'criterion' I was sure that Dr Conybeare was doomed. In fact I felt a very strong electrical surge as Dr Closer uttered the word 'criterion'. It was not simply that it was the *mot juste*, and that with it her victory was inevitable; but that, for the first time, I understood exactly what the word 'criterion' meant. You see, girls, I was only nineteen, and when you are young there are many words that you come across that you are not quite sure of, and you hope that you will discover exactly what they mean before someone finds you out. At that moment, for the first time in my life, listening to Dr Closer use the word, I knew exactly what the word 'criterion' meant: a 'criterion' was a test, principle or rule, a standard by which something is judged. And not only did I understand this word for the first time in my life, but I understood that Dr Closer had used the very lovely singular form of the plural term 'criteria', and that she had used it with great precision. Her slight pause before uttering it only added to the sense of revelation, and when the word came, exploding, as it were, onto the head of Dr Conybeare, and onto the assembled heads of her audience, I wanted to cry out loud, burst into applause, or shout at the top of my voice.

As above.

I HAVE perhaps given the impression, girls, that Dr Closer was an unsympathetic woman, but this was not at all the case. I really must try to make you understand. Dr Closer was in fact a very thoughtful, very perceptive, and very understanding woman. A very complex woman. Let me tell you another story which I think illustrates this.

It was around the same time as Hannah Closer appeared in front of me wearing only her underwear. I was at the Closer residence, and there was a boy there who was rather upset. I have no idea what he was doing there: he wasn't a student, nor was he, as far as I knew, any relation to Dr Closer. He would have been about fifteen or sixteen years old. He was slumped in a battered leather armchair in the living room of the Closer house – I'll get round to describing the Closer house in a moment, since it was quite unusual – and was delivering himself over and over again, with increasing bitterness, of the single word 'tarts'.

'Why do you call them "tarts"?' asked Dr Closer, who was sitting nearby smoking a cigarette.

'Because they *are* tarts,' the schoolboy replied. He looked utterly morose.

I should have mentioned that there was one other person present: Dr 'Goro' Fukushima, of Chiba University, the distinguished Japanese scholar and anglophile. He happened to be staying at the time with Dr Closer.

What happened next rather stuck in my mind. Dr Closer, who in the ordinary way was a ferocious champion of women's rights, and who would generally refuse to countenance a disparaging word such as 'tarts' – no matter who had uttered it – put out her hand and silently stroked the boy's arm. As she did this, she glanced at Dr Fukushima, on whose face, I was astonished to see, was a look of great sympathy – almost pain. Dr Fukushima, it seemed, understood the nature of the struggle that was taking place in the boy's soul, and pitied him. He obviously understood the meaning of the word 'tarts', or at least had deduced it from the context of the conversation. I looked again at Dr Closer. It was clear that Dr Closer knew that Dr Fukushima understood and pitied the boy; and moreover that both Dr Closer and Dr Fukushima were long familiar with the feelings the boy was experiencing, feelings as old as the hills, feelings that will persist in the breasts of boys and girls as long as we are all permitted to remain on this earth. Dr Closer recognized, I felt, that no homily on the correct use of language would ever address the real suffering of a boy rejected and humiliated by the young women he called 'tarts'; and so, instead of rebuking him, she merely looked, a little sadly and a little whimsically, at Dr Fukushima, while she stroked the boy's arm.

It was interesting to see the fleeting triangle of glances: Dr Closer, her eyes on Dr Fukushima; Dr Fukushima gazing with profound sympathy at the schoolboy; and the schoolboy scowling bitterly at the floor.

•

Reluctantly I will flag that for deletion too, although there is nothing really wrong with it, except possibly the use of the word 'tarts'.

Outside York somewhere.

THE SOUND of a door slamming as someone goes out, while you remain at home with nothing to do, is one of the most melancholy of all sounds. Especially when, after the slam, the house relapses into a deep, unbroken silence, like a sleep.

It was on one of these occasions, in the house in Christiania Street, that I was left in my room, rather ill. The room had a huge picture of a diplodocus on the wall. I remember a friend of mine, a young woman, coming round to look at it shortly after I had painted it: I took her up to my room and we spent some time examining it. After a time she said she liked it, but the head wasn't quite right. She was an interesting young woman: very tall, like a stork, and with a clever face. She was, I remember, forever reproving me with the words, 'Aren't you going to *do* something?' I remember being baffled by these words and being unable to find a reply. After all, why should I do anything? Isn't it enough that I exist? If you wish for something to be done, why don't *you* do it yourself, I wanted to say. But I can see that it is possible I was an irritating companion from her point of view: perhaps there *were* things I should have done, but didn't – and which it might have been expected I should have done. I remember one such occasion – when she delivered herself of these words – after we had been out on the town. It had been a rather unsatisfactory evening: the air had a very strange smell, the kind that one only finds in Hull. At any rate, we had returned, as I say, to her flat after this unsatisfactory evening. It was raining, and I was somewhat insufficiently dressed, as I always was in those days, with just a shirt that did nothing to keep off the freezing rain. We hastened inside. Once in her rooms she asked me to put on a record, which I did, and stood there listening to it in my wet shirt. Meanwhile she had made herself comfortable on the bed. And it was at that moment that she said 'Aren't you going to *do* something?'. I don't remember how the rest of the evening turned out. I think I might have left shortly afterwards, because I think that it might have been on that occasion that I caught pleurisy: you see, girls, how unwise it is to walk around all day and night half-starved and wearing a wet shirt. Yes, I think it was at that point that I went home, and it seems at least possible that it was on that occasion that I caught the cold that led ultimately to the illness that necessitated my leaving the university.

Or if it wasn't, it was a similar occasion. Anyway, to the point. The occasion I mentioned, a paragraph ago, when I heard the door slam and silence descend on the house... I was, as I have said, quite ill. My head was pounding and I was feverish. After a time I got up from my bed – just a mattress on the floor – and went out onto the landing. The hallway was rather desolate. The upstairs toilet door was open, and looking in I could see the toilet, the seat of which had been ripped off, so that one always had to perch over the cold and filthy rim. Some student prank, I expect. Everything in the hallway was filthy, and there was a pervasive decomposing smell. I don't know where that came from. I went stumbling down the stairs wrapped in all the clothes I had, to keep off the shivers. It was very cold. I had no idea where I was going or what I was doing. I may have been a little delirious. My mouth was full of a foul taste. Finally I stood in the ground floor hall, alone, in the silence of the house. The only light was a very faint glimmer from the road, through the panes of the front door. It was about four-thirty on an overcast December day, and if you are English – and you are English – you will know what that means. It was very, very dark and dim. The sun had set behind the clouds and night had fallen. Slimy black leaves lay in the streets. I stood in the hallway leaning against a stack of bicycles that almost blocked my way: there were six students in the house and each had a bicycle, so the hallway was rather full of them. In those days we used to cycle everywhere and were quite fit. So I stood there, really quite ill, clutching onto one of the cold metal frames and thinking, 'What should I do? What should I do?' There seemed to be nothing to do. There was no one to see, no one to talk to, no work to do, nothing to achieve, and nothing to look forward to tomorrow, except annihilation. It was, I will admit it, a moment of some despair – even of panic. And it was at that precise moment that I realised I was standing outside Madeleine's door. Madeleine was the girl I have mentioned, who had attempted to kick me in the groin. So, without thinking, I took the step over to the door and knocked on it.

A service station. About 8.30 or 9pm.

OUR COACH has just stopped again, for the third or fourth time. This time we've stopped at a service station.

Service stations are generally disliked, I believe. But why? These days they are generally clean and new-looking. There are places for children to play... There is the opportunity to buy just about anything. I've just been for a walk – the floors are really very highly polished – and had a good look around. I noticed an interesting coffee machine, of a type I've never seen before. It was quite enormous, brightly coloured, and covered with buttons and instructions. I didn't dare go near it, and certainly could never have plucked up the courage to order a coffee from it.

So I won't go as far as to say I *like* service stations; but I find the dislike with which they are often regarded is undeserved.

I leave aside the question of why service stations are disliked, even though it is interesting,* because I would like to discuss another subject. I, as you girls will know, am not exactly young. In fact I am forty-seven. Almost all of the other passengers, however, are much younger, as I have said – eighteen, nineteen or twenty years old – and moreover are mostly young women. Why discuss them? Well, they are quite interesting, I think. They are young, for a start. And as a group they are quite noticeably different from the general young

---

* Perhaps I could deal with this matter in a footnote. Service stations are, as I have said, generally clean, well-maintained, stocked with all sorts of necessary things, staffed by helpful people, and in fact specifically designed for the comfort and refreshment of the visitor. Why, then, do some people find – I have heard them say it – that when they enter these places they find themselves reacting, not with appreciation and satisfaction, but with a creeping malaise and disgust?

female population. Their clothes are different, their hair is different, their make-up is different, their gait is different.

Perhaps I could illuminate this subject by telling you what the young women were like when I was nineteen years old. This would have been in the early 1980s. For a start, they tended to wear damp woollen clothing. Their hair was messy, though not in a way that suggested they did not know it was messy. They wore very large boots, with thick soles. Many of them wore no make-up. They didn't seem very proud of their shape.

However, these girls (or young women) of *my* acquaintance back in the early 1980s were different from *ordinary* girls of the early 1980s. The ordinary fashionable girls would do their hair carefully, dye it, would wear make-up, short skirts, tights, and so on. The girls of my acquaintance were rather further out on the fringes of respectability. They were concerned with political matters such as the imminent destruction of the world, and were much preoccupied – rightly, in my view – with sexism, and certain other matters, and had a fondness for materials such as hemp. The ordinary young women of the town – those who were employed in jobs, for example – wouldn't have had anything to do with hemp. The willingness to employ materials such as hemp was a defining characteristic of the young women I was closely associated with.

The girls on this coach are their direct descendants. But something has happened in the last twenty years. These young women, although they show much kinship with the particular sub-group that I have attempted, I am afraid rather feebly, to describe (that is, the girls of my former acquaintance when I was nineteen), and, like them, don't wear much make-up, and are concerned with all sorts of ethical matters, and have the same highly disarranged hair – although they show kinship with them, as I say, they seem to have shed certain characteristics, and acquired new ones. For example, they no longer seem to wear the damp woollen clothing, and are much more comfortable with their own shape. But I won't dwell on that. They also have a tendency to wear jewellery in their mouths, noses and belly buttons. There was only one girl of my acquaintance when I was nineteen who had a nose-piercing, and she is now dead. Though that isn't of any relevance.

Still at the service station.

I HAVE been reading through what I have written so far, girls, and I am abashed to see that there are all sorts of loose ends dangling here and there. The more I go on, the more they seem to proliferate. Perhaps this method of mine, to scribble as fast as I can, is not such a good one. For example, the various young women. There is Guy, then Madeleine, then Hannah… and now this girl who died. There is also the girl who always used to say 'Aren't you going to *do* something?', who is not identical with the girl who died, though both are nameless.

But there is really no reason to worry. Everything, I promise, will become clear. I might, for example, give names to both of the nameless young women. The girl who says 'Aren't you going to *do* something?' is, I admit, quite an interesting character, in her way.

At this point I must, however, if I may (don't lose patience!) introduce one further character from my student days. And I can promise you, girls, that she will be very memorable. For a start, she had a memorable name – Aurora. Like the northern lights! Aurora was a quite beautiful creature, and I always felt on very friendly terms with her. In the presence of certain young women, it is natural for young men to feel a bit tongue-tied, due to their painful sense of being attracted – I apologize for this, girls, but it is probably best that you should know how men's minds work – but, in the presence of a true goddess, there is really nothing to worry about. She is as high above you as heaven is above earth, and there is no possibility of her falling in love with you or even taking much notice of you. You can therefore go about your business with her as if she were a marble statue, and you were examining her closely in a museum. You may even tell her to her face how beautiful she is. Perhaps she will find your candour refreshing, though of course she will be a little bored by you.

Well, let me describe her. Aurora was quite petite, with an oval face and very dark, almost raven hair, cut short at nape-length. Her eyes and eyelashes were very dark and lustrous, and her complexion was of the purest white. Her expression was that of a comfortable cat. Whenever she said anything, whatever it was, even something quite rude, it would come out so delightfully that you didn't mind it. You were happy to be spoken to. Despite her being quite untouchable, she had the reputation of having had many lovers. How true this was I don't know. However, I did have some direct experience in this regard. It was when I called on her one afternoon at her house in Pearson Park, one of the better neighbourhoods of Hull; a locale also inhabited, as it happened, by the poet Philip Larkin. The front door was answered by a friend of hers – this time I am afraid I cannot supply even the smallest biographical detail, so you may as well forget her – who said that Aurora was upstairs.

'Is she busy?' I asked.

The young woman thought a little. 'No, I don't think so,' she said.

'Can I just go up then?' I asked.

'Yes,' she said.

So I ran up the steps and knocked on Aurora's door. There was no answer. I pushed my way in. And there… but perhaps I shouldn't really describe what I saw. It is quite difficult now, even thinking about it.

Aurora, however, didn't seem in the least put out. She just looked up at me calmly. 'Yes?' she said. From downstairs I thought I heard the sound of laughter. I stumbled out some question... she answered me gravely...

Neither did the young man seem put out. It really was extraordinary.

So that was Aurora and I think I can guarantee that you will find it hard to forget her.

·

Unfortunately that will have to be cut. I am conscious that I am treading a fine line here. But children have a remarkable ability, I have noticed, to simply skate over things they don't understand – so I hope this will save me. Then again, perhaps they will be much older when they read this and as a result they will neither be shocked nor baffled.

I must just point out one other thing, while I am at it: unfortunately, despite what I said a few pages back, I do think, still, that there is reason to worry about the state of the world, which is obviously why I am on this coach. I would like my girls to be aware of the existence of weapons of mass destruction – at an appropriate age – but I don't want them to spend their entire youth worrying about them. Perhaps it would be better if they didn't read these diaries until they were considerably older – thirty or forty, say – and their best years were behind them. I certainly don't want to be responsible for blighting their lives.

This reminds me of a conversation I once had with Guy. We were at the university campus a couple of years ago – I had gone there for some reason and bumped into her. She was, if I recall correctly, distributing white poppies for peace for November 11th.

'How old were you,' she asked me, as we stood in the sunshine in the quad outside the Chaplaincy — it was November but really rather a beautiful day — 'when your parents told you about nuclear weapons?'

She seemed to assume that my parents had told me about nuclear weapons, when in fact they had not. I'd had to find out about their existence for myself. And I imagine that Guy was imagining my parents not just mentioning nuclear weapons, but having a good heart-to-heart talk with me about them, in all their aspects, political, economic, existential, and so on. In that moment I felt rather ashamed of my parents.

'I can't remember,' I replied.

'I was five,' she said, looking at me appraisingly.

Five!

That really is too young, I think.

Guy is an extraordinary person. As well as being quite extraordinarily persuasive and quite extraordinarily rude, depending on when you speak to her, she has several other notable characteristics. She reminds me of the young women of my acquaintance in the 1980s, in that her clothing is exclusively woollen. She rarely drinks tea or coffee, for reasons I have not yet been able to fathom. It may be because the tea or coffee has a long way to travel to reach these shores; or it may be that a certain amount of electricity is required to boil the kettle; or it may simply be that she doesn't think that tea and coffee are very good for her. If for the latter reason, then this may be what is responsible for her appearance of very good health. Although Guy is aged around twenty, she looks somewhat older. Her face is always well-scrubbed and rosy. Guy's face is very severe and I have never, in fact, seen her smile. It is of course quite possible that she smiles and laughs, even quite gaily, when I'm not there – when for example she is with those she loves – but I have never seen it happen. I am afraid Guy disapproves of me, though I have never been able to work out why. It has crossed my mind that it might be something to do with the Institute, but I cannot think quite what that might be.

I often attend the meetings chaired by Guy. At our last meeting, there were only four people in attendance: myself, an elderly German woman named Anna, another quite elderly woman named Prim, from the Hull region, and Guy herself. I once saw Prim at the Institute. Anna is a very congenial woman who works tirelessly at such activities as running stalls, collecting money for orphans, and sabotaging equipment at American airbases. Prim is a less congenial woman, though almost certainly an interesting person.

At this recent meeting we were, as usual, downstairs in the little shop that sells organic food and postcards, and were discussing the annual commemorations of the Hiroshima and Nagasaki bombings. The idea of these commemorations is to paint the shapes of people on the street in whitewash, representing the 'shadows' left by the people who were vaporized by the explosions. Last year this activity had been a resounding success. The police had, as usual, been highly co-operative, since the whitewash comes off at the first sign of rain. In fact, since the painting is done at night, the shadows are sometimes gone by the time people begin going about their business the following morning.

On the occasion of this recent meeting there was, I remember, another meeting in progress upstairs, over our heads. It was a campaigning group whose aim was to close down a vivisection laboratory in Cambridge. It was an extremely well-attended meeting – there must have been almost a hundred people packed up there. People were continually clattering up and down the stairs. Now, experimentation on animals is a troubling matter, girls; but I think it must rather have struck Guy and the two elderly ladies, as it certainly did me, how well attended the upstairs meeting was, compared to our own. Our meeting was concerned with nothing less than the destruction of the world, yet in comparison it was barely attended at all. Perhaps at that moment we four – though none of us articulated it – felt a slight draining-away of our spiritual resources, even some small nagging doubt about the relative worth of the two causes: the one, as I say, represented by an enormous conclave in the room upstairs, from which there was a continuous thudding of feet and scraping of chairs, and the other, by ourselves, rather diffident, rather cold, and rather hemmed in by rotary stands crammed with vegetarian recipe books.

At a pause in our deliberations, Anna suggested a cup of tea, and went to the sink under the stairwell.

'A cup of hot water, Guy?' she asked, a little timidly.

At that moment a tremendous drumming of feet and chorus of shouts was heard from above. Some motion had been passed. The Cambridge laboratory was to be destroyed utterly and razed to the ground.

I am not sure if Guy replied. If she did, whatever she said was drowned out by the noise.

IN ORDER to clear up the loose ends, I will just very briefly say something about the girl who died, the one who had a nose-piercing. Then we can get this narrative back on track. Her name was Alice. She was a young woman of about nineteen, with short hair dyed in a mixture of colours and with a small silver stud in the side of her nose, which, as I say, at the time was quite unusual. She often seemed to have a mischievous smile on her face. Alice also, now I come to think of it, had the reputation of having had many lovers. She had a remarkable philosophy. It was this: she made no distinctions among people because of their appearance.

As an example of this philosophy, let me tell you about a little thing I observed once: an incident involving Alice and one of our friends at the time, a young man of rather rough-hewn looks who had the nickname – bestowed by us in the cruelty of youth – of 'Garg', short for 'Gargoyle'. 'Garg' was in fact a charming fellow, but the girls of our acquaintance never took any notice of him and he was a little depressed, I think, as a result. 'Garg' was a giant of a young man, well over six feet tall, with enormous hands and feet and a huge, swollen and misshapen nose. He was very awkward and ungainly. I once saw Alice come into a room where 'Garg' was by himself in an armchair. I was chatting with a few friends. Alice immediately went over to 'Garg' – there was no necessity that she do so, since she could quite easily have joined the conversation in progress – and began talking to him. As far as I know she had never met him until that moment. I don't know what the outcome of the conversation was, if any, but it seemed to me a remarkable act.

Unfortunately, as I have said, Alice died, though much later, in her thirties. She threw herself off a bridge. She was last seen standing on the rail of the walkway, clutching a doll. The witness was a young man who was up early, walking his dog. It was a misty morning in winter. He approached her to try to say a few words, but Alice leapt from the rail into the icy river and was seen no more.

Tadcaster.

WELL, THE coach has stopped again. We seem to be stopping everywhere. I think this is Tadcaster.

Some more girls are getting on. The coach is now full of young women, all laughing and chatting. 'Beaver' is about the only other male on the coach besides myself. He is seated at the back and occasionally his voice booms out. I am sitting about halfway up, on the left-hand side. It would be nice if someone came and talked to me, but as it is I am content for now. I must look rather odd to them. For a start, I am wearing a suit. I don't know why I do these things – after all, a suit makes me stick out like a sore thumb. Why am I wearing a suit when they are so casual? They are all in jeans and sturdy boots (the boots are for practical reasons, since we shall be standing in the cold, and possibly the wet), and have exposed midriffs. Doubtless they have sensible raincoats in their bags. Their hair, sometimes braided, sometimes loose, sometimes done in a style I cannot really describe, falls in great luxuriant masses over their shoulders, which in some cases are also exposed. By the way, I have recently begun to notice a difference between the hair of young women and that of old women. The hair of old women is thinner and less substantial, and of course is more apt to be grey, or else it is dyed so as not to show the grey. It is also more apt to be cut short. The hair of very old women is apt to be extremely fine and thin, almost like threads of cotton wool. It has very little volume. But these young girls have hair with a very great deal of volume.

Just over the aisle from me are two girls who seem more serious than some of the other girls on the coach.

They appear to be spending their time reading. One of them, the one nearest to me, is, I think, Chinese. If I wanted to, I could exchange a few words with her in her native language. Her hair puts me in mind of new tarmac: it is very black and shiny. She is wearing a checked jacket. Out of the corner of my eye I can see that she is also wearing, underneath, a top that looks a bit like a nightdress, or night-top, in very light pink, so light as to be almost white, silky and with forlorn straps in front. Strands of jet-black hair are carelessly falling over it. This garment terminates at her waist, revealing a small strip of flesh. Below that, biting into the flesh, is a pair of white trousers.

There is one other male on the coach apart from 'Beaver'. From where I am sitting, I can just see his head poking up a few seats in front of me. He is an ex-doctor called Tim. He is wearing a leather coat of antique vintage, and has not shaved for a good while. When I came past him I noticed he had a magazine on the seat next to him. One of the headlines read: 'Dropped Soap Accounts for 90% of Toe Fractures.' I think someone mentioned to me that Tim is a recovering alcoholic. I would say he is about my age – in his mid forties. His face has a sunken look. I have never had a conversation of any length with him, but I am sure he would be an interesting conversationalist. I think he is asleep at the moment. His head seems to have nodded to the side.

As above.

'GARG' WAS a student of engineering, I think.

As above.

It's GETTING quite late.

I have just remembered a rather amusing incident to do with Alice. This won't take a moment, and, if you wish, you can skip forward. Alice was a friend of another young man called Daniel. Daniel was a couple of years older than most of the rest of us — he would have been about twenty-three — but had delayed going to university for a few years, I think to work abroad. He always wore a blazer covered with small badges. Daniel, in addition to being a friend of Alice, claimed also to have lived a previous life with her in ancient Egypt, where she had been a queen and he a palace servant. Daniel was capable of telling you this sort of nonsense in a very grave manner, as if bestowing an important confidence on you. If you tried to protest that it was obviously all a fantasy of his, he would look at you in a puzzled fashion. 'I am disappointed in you,' he would seem to be saying. 'I thought you were a person of some imagination.'

It was Daniel who introduced us to Alice. It happened as follows. One early evening in winter, Daniel dropped by at the house at Christiania Street, where we were all watching television. Among those present were myself, Henry, the young man whose name I can't remember, a young man called 'Dick' (his last name was Dixon), the girlfriend of 'Dick', and a couple of other girls and boys. I think 'Garg' was there. Daniel popped his head round the door and said hello. There was a small stir of interest when we saw that he had a young woman with him: Alice. Daniel introduced her. After exchanging a few words we all went back to watching television. Daniel and Alice found a spot on the floor and began to watch the programme with us.

After about ten minutes I began to notice something. Daniel and Alice were sitting next to 'Dick' and the girlfriend of 'Dick' on the floor; and as I watched – I was behind Alice, Daniel, 'Dick' and the girlfriend of 'Dick' – I saw that Alice had put her hand out and was lightly caressing the fingers of 'Dick'. I should reiterate that 'Dick' had never met Alice, and nor had Alice met 'Dick': in fact she had never met any of the people in the room. This is important for what follows.

After a while I saw that 'Dick' had moved a little closer to Alice, and was caressing her fingers in return: nothing much, just a light mingling of hands. Then he began to touch her hair. It was probably at that point that everyone in the room noticed that something very odd was going on. The girlfriend of 'Dick' noticed it too, of course, since she was sitting right next to 'Dick'; but she affected not to notice. Soon the caresses and touches between Alice and 'Dick' had grown more overt. They exchanged a kiss. Still we all simply continued to watch television as if nothing was happening. Then 'Dick' and Alice slipped to the carpet, and began rolling around; and in fact the girlfriend of 'Dick' had to move a little to get out of their way. She was still studiously ignoring them. After about two or three minutes of this, 'Dick' and Alice picked themselves up and, hand in hand, walked out of the room. Everyone ignored them as they left. I should stress the fact that it was all done in absolute silence. The television was the only commentary.

You will think that this could not possibly have happened, girls, but I assure you it is true. To be completely frank I found it all rather nasty. I felt terribly sorry for the girlfriend of 'Dick'. Daniel, however, I did not feel sorry for. He wasn't bothering to conceal a tiny expression – barely perceptible – of quiet pleasure. For some reason, it seemed, he had wanted this to happen.

·

Obviously that will have to be cut. I will mark it. But I wanted to get it off my chest. And now I have done so, I can see that it isn't at all amusing, and in fact the whole thing makes me feel sick. Not so much for myself, but for the girlfriend of 'Dick'. I didn't know her, and in fact never discovered her name, but I could clearly imagine what she was feeling. She hadn't been able to find either the words or the actions to intervene; didn't know whether she even had the right *to intervene; was unsure whether or not everyone would laugh at her if she did or said anything. So she remained silent, and suffered, while Alice, with terrible skill, stole 'Dick' away from her and in fact walked off with him. The girlfriend of 'Dick' was left alone in utter ignominy. No one wished to speak to her; no one even wished to acknowledge what had happened.*

After a time the girlfriend of 'Dick' slank out. Again, remarkably, she didn't say anything to anyone, and no one said anything to her. We were all shamefaced. She just left the room, then left the house and went home, doubtless to weep on her bed. At the time I didn't consider going after her. I felt inadequate to the task. I probably wondered whether if I did go after her and say something, she would turn on me and vent all her shame and suffering onto me.

I should have helped the girlfriend of 'Dick'; should perhaps have said a kind word to her or done something. But the truth was that we were all glad to get rid of her. When she had gone, the house was purged of the evil that had been done. Except, perhaps, for the continuing presence of Daniel. Daniel was still there, still watching television.

Shortly afterwards I left too; I went upstairs and lay on my mattress.

Past Leeds: we didn't stop at Leeds.

THE WEAPONS held at Faslane would be enough by themselves to destroy the earth twice over. *By themselves.* I remember quoting that statistic one morning, to a woman who, in my childhood, I had called my aunt. Her response was to say this: 'Someone's been reading the *Guardian.*' I was a little hurt by this, since I was very fond of her, but I soon realised that she was simply making a joke – she had a smile on her face. Strange to say, it was Christmas morning.

•

I'm afraid I haven't organized myself very well. I haven't brought with me any wet-weather clothing. It's important to prepare for all eventualities, but this time, unaccountably, I left home with just what I'm standing up in – viz., my suit. I was probably a bit flummoxed by Guy's call. I just agreed, knowing (in my heart of hearts) that it wasn't a very good day to drop everything and go to Scotland. For one thing, I had a lot of work to do. The Institute is preparing to welcome Professor Wo, of Sai Kun University, who will be arriving next week to favour us with a talk. The result was that I had no time to prepare properly. I didn't even have time to make a packed lunch. The day seemed fine, and I very foolishly trusted to luck that it would continue so. The wet-weather clothing is at the bottom of a drawer somewhere. And now I can see spots of rain on the window.

•

A WORD about the Institute. The Institute was set up in 1985, largely through my own efforts and that of a couple of colleagues with an interest in the Chinese language. One of these, in fact, was a fellow student: the very Rod who had been attacked so savagely by Dr Closer for fiddling with his pencil case. He recovered completely from the experience.

The main objective of the Institute is to foster mutual cultural understanding between China and Britain, which we achieve via our monthly 'Third Wednesday' talk, open to members of the public. Refreshments are supplied.

All sorts of strange people come along to the talks. Some of them seem to be – frankly – quite lunatic. I've often wondered why they turn up. Perhaps they come for the refreshments.

Most of the time I sleep at the Institute. As its founder I have my own room there.

A WORD more about Daniel and Alice. You may be wondering whether Daniel was Alice's boyfriend, and if so, why he didn't mind her going off with 'Dick'. In fact, it's possible I may have to cut the entry above featuring Daniel, Alice, 'Dick' and the girlfriend of 'Dick', and will therefore have to cut this one too. For now, I'll let it stand, though. I'll review it later.

Actually I have no real idea, especially after all this time, why Daniel simply sat there and let Alice do what she did. Was it because Daniel had some animus against the girlfriend of 'Dick'? Was that why there was a little smile playing over his face as Alice walked out of the room with 'Dick'? Did Daniel plan the whole thing, in fact, with Alice as his confederate? Was his purpose to humiliate the girlfriend of 'Dick'? Had she hurt him in some way? I know nothing about the girlfriend of 'Dick' at all, not even her name – which is why I have to keep referring to her in this ludicrous way – and can't even remember much about her appearance, except that she was a redhead. If so – if Daniel wished somehow to get his revenge on the girlfriend of 'Dick' – then this could well be the explanation for the whole thing. Three people come out of this story very badly, therefore: Daniel, for devising the plan; Alice, for agreeing to go along with it; and 'Dick', for mindlessly submitting to Alice's overtures, in front of his own girlfriend. The poor girlfriend of 'Dick' was overwhelmed by the combined malignity of three people. Why? What had she done to deserve it? And how suddenly it all descended on her! One moment she was watching television, and the next – without a word being spoken – her life was destroyed. And no one helped, no one said a word!

But possibly it is time to turn to other topics.

I HAVE realised that you still have no real idea who Madeleine was – and after all she is the most important person in all of this.

Well, as you know, Madeleine was the girl who lived in the front room of our shared house in Hull. It was Madeleine who wore the shapeless orange dress and boots, and who tried to deal me a blow that evening in the kitchen. On the night when I was sick with a sort of spiritual malaise in the hallway, it was Madeleine's room that I found myself outside: and it was on Madeleine's door that I knocked.

When I first met her, Madeleine was in her third year at the university, studying social sciences. She was, therefore, about two years older than I. At the time of our first meeting – when I began my studies at the university, and began living in the shared house in Christiania Street – she would have been twenty-one, and I nineteen.

Madeleine was Scottish, from Barra, in the Hebrides. Perhaps that explains her fiery temper.

When I knew her, Madeleine was not beautiful, but neither was she ugly. She was very far from ugly, in fact. She once confessed to me that she thought she had big ears, but I never myself thought so. To me they seemed quite normally-sized. She had lovely dark eyes and soft, curling dark hair.

In fact I must take back that remark about the big ears: you'll think that she really did have big ears, and that I'm refusing to recognize them out of gallantry. But they really were not big. Perhaps I should try to correct this impression by going to the opposite extreme, thus:

in fact they were very small. Now, hopefully, you will be left with a mental impression of ears that are neither noticeably large nor small.

Similarly, I have just said that she was not beautiful. That, now I come to think of it, is also a travesty. I should simply delete that sentence. In fact, she was very beautiful. She was not as beautiful as Aurora, but then Aurora, as everyone would admit, was quite mind-bogglingly beautiful. Madeleine's was a more ordinary style of beauty. Actually most girls at the age of twenty-one are beautiful. Anyway, this is rather dull.

All right, I will try harder: facially, Madeleine's features were distinctive. Her eyebrows were thick and dark, and her eyes were large and seemed to slope at the corners. She sometimes looked a little Spanish, though her skin was not at all dark. Her lips were often compressed with a thoughtful expression. She was of medium height, but sturdy. Madeleine's hair, as I have mentioned, was dark, and she smelled of night-flowering jasmine. If that sounds unlikely, I assure you it is true. I have had many opportunities since to smell night-flowering jasmine – it has a waxy, syrupy, rich aroma – and it is remarkably similar to the bloom of Madeleine's skin. She sometimes wore the orange dress: at other times she wore a black dress. She rarely wore jeans. When she walked in the house – for example if she was going from one side of the kitchen to the other – she had a peculiar tiptoe gait that was very endearing. On reflection, perhaps she didn't really tiptoe – it was just that the way she threw her weight forward made her look as if she was walking on tiptoe. After all, with the heavy boots she wore, it would be difficult to walk on tiptoe. Yet when she walked outside, this mannerism disappeared and she walked entirely normally.

Madeleine was – and, I imagine, still is – a person of strong convictions. She had a strong social sense. She was much concerned to defend the rights of animals, and women. She was a vegetarian. She was also a highly spiritual person.

Perhaps I should now describe what happened when I knocked on the door that afternoon.

As soon as I knocked I heard the faint creaking of bed springs. After a time the door opened a crack and I saw Madeleine's face. She saw me, and her brows contracted a little.

'Oh,' she said. 'It's you.'

I had never glimpsed her room and was rather startled by what I saw through the crack. It was glowing with all sorts of warm colours: rugs and throws and wall-hangings and cushions in red and orange and yellow. From the cold and dark hallway it looked wonderfully inviting.

'I was wondering,' I said, not really knowing what I was going to say, 'if I could talk to you.'

I must just say at this point that I had never done anything like this before and had no idea what to expect from it. It felt very strange.

Madeleine opened the door wider. 'Come in, then,' she said.

I knew that I had disturbed her, but I was terribly grateful to be invited in – I say terribly because my gratitude at that moment was literally terrible, flooding my head and neck. I was very ill. So I went in and, looking around, sat on the floor.

'No,' Madeleine said, pointing to a large, bright

orange cushion covered in sequins. I sat on the cushion and said nothing: the room was so warm I immediately felt like going to sleep. The whole room smelled of night-flowering jasmine.

Madeleine sat on the sofa and picked something up. It was a woollen thing – in fact a piece of knitting. Without looking at me particularly, she started knitting it: she didn't seem embarrassed by my presence, and nor did she ask what I had come for. You must remember that my last contact, my very last, with her, had been when I had danced with her around the kitchen, and she had walked into the night.

I, for my part, didn't say anything. It felt good just to be in the room, in the silence, listening to the jets of the gas fire. I moved the cushion slightly along the floor so I could rest my back on the wall. I powerfully wanted to sleep. Madeleine's needles clicked. At that moment, very strangely, it was as if we were an old married couple. I suddenly felt very familiar with the room, even though I had never been in it – with the little stove that Madeleine kept clean and tidy (that explained why she visited the communal kitchen so rarely), and with Madeleine herself. I imagined that we had grown so used to one another that we both knew one another's opinions about everything and no longer had anything to say to one another, whereas in fact the opposite was true – we knew next to nothing about one another, and had everything to say.

'What did you want to talk about?' Madeleine asked suddenly.

'Nothing,' I replied, opening my eyes. 'I'm sorry... I just wanted to say hello. Shall I go?'

'*No...*' she said, looking at me carefully. 'Are you well?'

'Yes, I think so,' I replied.

'You're trembling,' she said. 'Are you frightened?'

'No,' I replied.

'Are you drugged on something?'

'No.'

'Then you have a fever. You should really go to bed. Or call a doctor.'

'I do feel a bit odd,' I said. 'I think I might have eaten something that disagreed with me.'

'I'm not surprised,' Madeleine said. (I think she must have been referring to the kitchen, which was not in a state of very good repair. The oven was virtually unusable, for example. Someone had tried roasting onions in it and it couldn't be turned on without emitting clouds of black smoke.)

'I did want to say something,' I said.

Madeleine was silent, though her needles continued to click.

'If I could just stay a moment…' I ventured. 'I won't stay long.'

'You can stay until I've finished this,' Madeleine said, indicating her knitting. 'But I really think you should go to bed.'

That was enough. First I would gather my forces, I thought, and then I would say what I wanted. I would apologize, for a start, for my behaviour. I would make her see that I was not the kind of man who treats women… in *that* way. I sat with my head against the wall and in a few moments I began to doze. I knew that I had to stop myself, to arrest the doze and begin the explanation… but I was falling further and further into unconsciousness. I was in fact extremely ill, perhaps even a little delirious.

I think near Ripon.

IT'S NOW drizzling in earnest. The sun set long ago.

Outside, the country is flat. There are a lot of long, low fields stretching out in the gloom. Occasionally a building flashes past. One very unusual one came past just now – a pet crematorium. It had a huge illuminated sign. I suppose pets need to be cremated as well as humans. I've never really thought about it. A hamster or a canary I suppose you could just bury in your back garden, but a dog – especially a large one – would need quite a big grave; and so I suppose that's the reason. I've never had a dog or a cat. I'm a little allergic to them. But I like dogs very much. I remember once, Madeleine and I were by the lake at theuniversity – this was when we had an understanding, of sorts. It was June, I think, and a man came past with a big, floppy dog and it bounded over to us in a friendly way. We were sitting on a bench. Madeleine likes dogs, and she put her hand out to stroke it, but, strange to say, the dog seemed more interested in me. That's often the way with animals – they are more interested in the people who don't like them – though, as I've said, it isn't that I don't like dogs: I don't particularly like touching them, and there is a certain thing… It is rather awkward, but I don't think I would ever be able to follow a dog around with a plastic bag. I greatly appreciate it when I see owners doing that for their dogs, because it is a highly responsible thing to do, and it is particularly important for children not to encounter the waste products of dogs – with children one is always scraping things off their shoes and telling them 'Don't walk there –' or 'Watch out – mind your step!' So this man was behaving very responsibly. Come to think of it though I don't think he had a plastic bag. Anyway, the dog bounded over, as I said, and buried its muzzle in my lap in the rather insistent and nosing way that some dogs have. It was quite strong, I remember. It was a floppy sort of dog but it was in the prime of life, and it dug itself in quite fiercely. The situation was rather embarrassing. It was also a very strange sensation. After all, I didn't know if it would bite. I felt fairly confident it wouldn't, but what if it had? Madeleine, to my surprise, began laughing. The man who was walking the dog came over. He was a nondescript sort of chap — middle-aged, perhaps fifty, balding, and running to fat, but with a pleasant expression.

'He's only being friendly,' he said.

'Please can you tell him to stop?' I asked.

The man came forward and took hold of the dog's collar — it wasn't on a lead. 'Come on,' he said to the dog, and pulled it out of my lap.

I looked down. A most astonishing sight met my eyes. The dog had left a big river of slobber all over my trousers. It was quite astonishing, the amount of slobber the dog had produced in such a short time. Perhaps it had been saving it up during its walk and had simply expelled it onto me when it put its head in my lap. I was absolutely covered in it. It was like whipped cream, though slightly more translucent. It lay in great streaks all over the tops of my legs, and in between, where its snout had been resting. I must have given a cry — I think I stood up — and the man looked at me. Strange to say I remember quite well the expression on his face. Normally it is difficult to remember something as evanescent as an expression after many years have passed — and this was easily twenty-seven years ago — but I recall clearly that he seemed to be asking me: 'What on earth are you worried about?' Actually that doesn't quite do justice to it. He seemed to be saying this, as follows: 'I see you are standing up as if there's something wrong. Whatever it is I'm sorry, but of course I myself and my dog have nothing to do with it. However, I recognize that it takes all sorts to make a world, and so I will just leave now and I bid you good-day.'

I turned to Madeleine and she was looking at me – it is fortunate I suppose that I wasn't with the young woman who had the habit of saying 'Aren't you going to *do* something?', as I expect that would be what she would have said in the circumstances – and the remarkable thing was that Madeleine was looking at me in much the same way as the man with the dog had done, as if it was really nothing untoward that I had been covered with slobber. 'Why don't you calm down?' would perhaps have been an accurate transcription of her expression, though she too, of course, did not actually say those words.

Meanwhile, I had nothing to brush the slobber off with. The man simply walked away with his dog, and, there being nothing else to do, I sat back down again, rather heavily. But at that moment the dog broke free from its owner and bolted straight back for me, burying its nose, like a rocket, right in my groin. This time it was all too much, especially when I saw that the dog had left another long trail of white sticky slobber all up my thigh. 'Get this dog off me!' I shouted – or something similar. Again the owner came back, again took the dog by the collar, and again walked off with it, the dog straining all the while to get back at me. On the man's face there was now another expression, similar to the first one but this time subtly altered. Now he seemed to be saying: 'Really, you are making a fuss about nothing, aren't you? What a peculiar specimen you are.' This unexpected coda to the performance had thrown Madeleine into a fit of giggles. And as the man walked away he delivered himself of a comment over his shoulder. It was this: 'Some people just don't like dogs.'

Perhaps I shouldn't have gone into so much detail, girls, but the sight of the pet crematorium reminded me of the incident.

On the A1 to Darlington.

In the end Madeleine went back to Scotland, where I understand she now works for the police service in some capacity. If she did join the police, that would have been an excellent career choice. I have always supported the police. And why not? They do excellent work. Surely an efficient police force is essential to the smooth running of any society. Would we wish to be without a police force? In my dealings with the police I have always found them to be courteous and fair.

Strange to say, I visited Barra when a child, on holiday with my parents. My granddad came too, but he broke his ankle and had to be airlifted to the mainland. I suppose I would have been about eight. I have confused memories of that holiday. I am convinced, in some portion of my mind, that I and some local children got caught up in an adventure which involved a collie dog. However, this must be either a dream, or something influenced by my reading of *The Famous Five*. I was very young at the time, and my memories before the age of about thirteen are extremely unreliable.

Past Darlington.

AFTER THAT experience in Madeleine's room I became very ill indeed. I never did tell Madeleine what I wanted to, and found, when I woke up, that I wasn't in her room, but in my bedroom, with a doctor bending over me. It was then, I am sure, that I was forced to leave the university. Yes: because immediately after that afternoon in Madeleine's room I spent two weeks in hospital. I had pneumonia, influenza and pleurisy, all at once, and the doctor, an old man whose eyelids were held up with surgical tape, said that although it was quite difficult to distinguish each from the other, each, to an experienced eye, was certainly present. The pleurisy was the most painful. The pleurae are the membranes that enfold each lung, and if they become inflamed, as they do in pleurisy, the lungs press painfully against the inflamed tissue. Charlemagne died of pleurisy, as did the poet Tsuen Wan. It must be a very painful death, combining physical agony with slow asphyxiation.

I also had, during that time, tremendous headaches. On one occasion I remember sitting up in my hospital bed when a middle-aged couple came in to see their son, who was in the bed next to mine. They smiled at me and said: 'You seem a lot better today.' It emerged that on their previous visit I had been moaning loudly – and, doubtless, disturbing them. I, however, could remember nothing.

After the two weeks in hospital, I was booked into a convalescent home called St Osyth's Priory, on the Essex coast.

St Osyth's had the faintly patchwork air that long-neglected properties often have. The floors and ceilings were cracked, there was a lot of ingrained dirt, and much restoration with chipboard had taken place. This did not detract from its considerable virtues, however. For example, the house was set in a large park with ancient gardens. There were deer in these gardens, quite tame, and in the mornings they would come right up and nibble the grass outside my bedroom window. St Osyth's seemed remote from the troubles of the world, and for the first time in a long while I was able to relax. My Chinese improved enormously: I had my Han cards with me and was working my way through them. I became quite good friends with a chap called Martin who, it seemed, had been involved in some sort of accident. He had been in Malaya, I think. Martin only had one leg.

One other thing I would like to mention: about a week after my arrival, the chambermaid asked if I would like to 'go out' with her daughter.

This came right out of the blue. The chambermaid was tidying my room one morning, and I was still there, pottering around, about to go down for breakfast. This chambermaid was a short, stout woman. I think she and her daughter were both of Italian extraction. I said no, thank you: I'd seen the girl and she was very attractive, but I didn't think I was quite strong enough. The truth was that I was still too much in love with Madeleine.

The chambermaid didn't bother me again. It occurred to me to recommend Martin in my place, but on reflection I decided to leave the decision to her.

As above.

I MUST just add, at this point, something further about the girl who always used to say, 'Aren't you going to *do* something?' I'm going to just dash this off, just to get it down. I have the strong feeling that she was in love with me, though she never said as much. I suppose I should have treated her more sensitively. Shortly after that occasion in her room, she acquired a new boyfriend. Of course, this doesn't necessarily indicate anything, but I suspect that it was an attempt on her part to make me see that she was desirable. I would not even advance this idea if I did not strongly suspect it to be true. The reason I say this is that one afternoon she turned up at my house with the boyfriend himself, a young man with a black beard, and brought him up to my room (the one with the diplodocus). I remember the young man with the black beard lounging on my mattress – this was before I had bought a proper bed – and gazing at me without speaking. Then, after the two of them had been there for a short time, they took their leave. It was almost as if the young woman who always used to say, 'Aren't you going to *do* something?' was now trying to say to me, 'Now you have seen him, we'll be off.' I felt a little sorry for her, and sensed her dislike of me. You girls will probably be surprised to learn that it is quite possible to be in love with someone and actively dislike them at the same time. I never saw her again, not even at the university, despite the fact that she was on the same course as I was – oriental languages. Mind you, I dropped out after only one term.

This is all I can remember about the young woman who always said 'Aren't you going to *do* something?' I now realize that this is a terrible disappointment. I am racking my brains, but there are no memories of her beyond the ones I have told you about. If only I could remember her name, or even something else that she once said, anything, apart from 'Aren't you going to *do* something?' She seemed so promising as a character yet now she has evaporated into nothing.

·

Good God! I *have* remembered something! I swear to you, girls, that I wasn't making it up just now when I said I had forgotten everything. Yet now something has just come back to me, completely unexpectedly. And it is actually quite interesting.

·

I have just realised that although it is quite interesting I don't really wish to share it on these pages. Rather frustrating. But I must just mention what it was. Actually, it is rather anodyne. It is as follows. It was on that evening when we went out together, and I got soaked in the rain. We had been to a dance, the sort of disco one used to find everywhere in the 1980s: a rather dismal affair. There were a few young people from the town there, but the place was half empty. I began dancing, I think probably in a rather unskilful way. I could feel the eyes of the young woman who always said 'Aren't you going to do *something?' on me, but as I was rather drunk, I simply continued to dance in this jerky, unskilful and rather foolish way, as if I was dancing not for my own pleasure, but to spite somebody; perhaps even to spite her, the girl who always said 'Aren't you going to* do *something?' The music was loud and echoing, and the floor was sticky. After a time the girl who always said 'Aren't you going to* do *something?' leaned close to me and shouted in my ear – it was impossible to be heard without shouting – 'You're beautiful!'*

It was the first and in fact I think the only time anyone has ever said those exact words to me. I felt a small sense of triumph, mingled with weariness, much as, I imagine, Aurora, the beautiful young woman, usually felt, on hearing a similar declaration. I didn't respond in any other way except to keep dancing. Then the young woman who always said 'Aren't you going to do something?' leaned over again, and shouted 'Take it or leave it!'

It is quite astonishing that I have just remembered all this, after all these years. Now it seems that the young woman who always said 'Aren't you going to do something?' no longer really deserves that epithet, since she made two other recorded utterances. I speak of exact utterances, since, as I have mentioned above, I do remember the gist of some remarks she once made about the head of the diplodocus on my bedroom wall. Yet, ironically, just at the point when the epithet 'the girl who always said "Aren't you going to do something"' no longer strictly applies, I have to leave her forever, since I am quite sure that at this point there is nothing, literally nothing, that I can remember about her.

·

Except – good God! This is really remarkable. I have just remembered one other thing she said.

Durham bus station.

I'VE ALSO just remembered something about the chambermaid's daughter I told you about earlier on, and perhaps I will get this down first, if you don't mind. I apologize for the digression, girls, but if I don't write it down now I will forget it. Yes: something rather odd happened a few days *before* her mother made the offer I mentioned.

I was in my room at the Priory when there was a knock on the door. I was standing at the washbasin holding a piece of soap. When I heard the knock, I put the piece of soap up to my mouth as if to eat it. It was one of those very small, paper-wrapped tablets – the type you often find in hotel bathrooms – and I had just unwrapped it. Presumably the act of unwrapping, combined with the sudden interruption, had suggested to my unconscious that I raise it to my lips, like a piece of white chocolate. And while I was standing there with the soap held to my lips, the chambermaid's daughter came in without waiting for an answer. I'm sure she entered like that deliberately. She was, as I have said, quite attractive, about eighteen, with shoulder-length chestnut hair, and with a nice shape. She was carrying some towels. When she saw me with the soap six inches from my mouth, and with my mouth half open as if to receive it, she laughed merrily. It was a very pleasant laugh, but I'm afraid I was dreadfully confused, and blushed. She then said 'Excuse me', put a towel down and left.

The following day I encountered her in the corridor outside my room, just as I was leaving. She was once again holding a pile of linen – sheets, I think – which she had just taken from a trolley.

68

'Hello,' she said in her Italian accent. 'I'm sorry about it. When I came into your room.'

'That's all right,' I said.

'Can I make your bed now?' she asked.

'Yes, please do,' I said.

She came past me and as she did so she looked at me very coquettishly.

In fact I have not told the entire truth about this incident.

Still in Durham bus station. The driver seems to have disappeared. Most of the girls are asleep. I regret to say that no one has come to sit next to me.

THE PUNGENT, plastic smell of Hull made me long occasionally for the woods around Ash Hill, where my parents lived, in Bournemouth. This house, my parental home, where I had grown up, was a detached property with a large garden. Behind it were the woods, and looming over them, the bald crown of Ash Hill itself with its three poplars, sticking up like cricket stumps. In that first year at Hull – before my parents died – I would often make the journey back to Bournemouth, because I loved the woods and drew a great deal of comfort from them.

I realise that I haven't mentioned this before, but I suppose I didn't really want to talk about it. So I will just say it. My father had a heart attack in the March of 1982, which killed him; and my mother also died, shortly afterwards, in circumstances that I will not go into at the moment. So both your paternal grandparents, girls, were now dead.

(As I write, one of the girls on the coach has put on a radio, which, although she is wearing earphones, is quite audible. At this time of night, when people are sleeping, this is a little inconsiderate. Ah. It has stopped. Oh – and started again. However, I will go on as best I can.)

One day, probably in the October of 1981 or thereabouts, I was at home in Bournemouth in the afternoon watching a Norman Wisdom comedy. Norman Wisdom was involved in a prize-giving

70

ceremony in which a number of dignitaries had assembled on a stage in the open air. At one point the stage collapsed and the dignitaries all took a tumble. And just at that point I heard a sound from outside.

It is probably difficult for you girls to imagine the terror we felt during the 1980s at the sound of an early-warning siren. It was, after all, the herald of the end of the world. The siren was on top of the police station, about half a mile away, and it was very loud. The police were in the habit of testing it by letting it run for one half-oscillation, that is, from the peak of the siren's pitch, downward until it had died away. That was frightening enough, but on this occasion the siren failed to die away and kept going.

Immediately I stood up, the film forgotten. My heart was hammering against my ribs. It was not a test. This could only mean one thing. It was the end of the world.

I knew exactly what it was I had to do: I had to go to the top of Ash Hill and die up there. If I stood exposed on the hill I would be killed instantly, and that was preferable to being buried in the rubble of the house. I have always had a horror of that – which is why I always feel very nervous when visiting China, because of the earthquakes.

Accordingly I left the house, leaving the front door open – I was dimly aware that I was holding something but I threw it away from me – and quickly walked the few yards to the fence that bordered the common land leading to the top of the hill. I remember clearly that I walked rather than ran. I think, even at that moment, I was a little embarrassed that someone might see me panicking. I hopped over the fence and began walking as fast as I could up the hill, over the rough ground.

With every step I felt that the ground might explode beneath my feet. The siren was still howling away. It was very loud.

Ash Hill rises quite sharply from the northern part of Bournemouth and is easily the highest point for miles around. Our house was already halfway up it, so it wasn't long before I got to the top of the hill – under two minutes, I would say. From there I could see the whole of Bournemouth spread out before me. There was nothing to do now except wait. I simply stood there, listening to the siren, not so much with my ears, as with my nerves, skin and flesh. I was shivering and I felt sick. My heart was still pounding. I had turned to face away from the town, north, into the area of likely detonation. I felt somehow that it was best to face the explosion.

By now the siren had completed about seven or eight ululations. There was no one about on top of the hill except, about fifty yards away, an old man, walking his dog. No one had come to join me to die in the open air. Instead they cowered in their houses. The siren continued howling like a wild beast... I waited for death. Eight ululations, nine, ten... the old man too seemed to be waiting for something... Was he here for the same reason as I? I hadn't noticed him running up the hill: had he been here already? Why was he loitering on the brow of the hill, as I was? Did he, too, understand, and wish for a rapid death?

Then, unexpectedly, on the thirteenth or fourteenth ululation, the siren swooped down, growled, and then lay there, exhausted, unable to rise. Silence. There had been no explosion. What did it mean?

I glanced at the old man. Surely, if an attack were still expected, the siren would have continued? Was it a false alarm? Could it really mean we were to be spared? The old man was walking in meditative circles. He seemed to be slowly getting nearer. He was coming over. He was a little old man in a soft cap.

'It's all go today,' he said.

And it was at this point, with great waves of joy and relief, that I realised that the danger was past. There was to be no attack. It was some sort of mistake. Perhaps, girls, one day you will feel as I did then. I had another hour, day, week, month to live. I felt bathed in bliss. I felt a sudden, intense love for the old man: he seemed remarkably handsome.

Without saying anything to him – I couldn't speak – I ran down the hill, not looking back.

I still think of that old man now and then, and his remark. It was, in a way, the perfect remark. There was a wry humour in it. There was an affirmation of our common humanity in the face of the powerful and malign forces ranged against us. Yet there was also humility. It was not grandiose.

When I got home I saw what it was that I had thrown away from me as I left the house. It was a metal teaspoon. I'd ripped it in half as I left the house and thrown it onto the front path. The two halves were lying there. I picked them up and examined them. What power in my hands! Not merely to bend metal, but to rip it apart! And without even knowing I'd done it!

You will ask yourselves whether this is possible, girls. But it is possible. It really happened. The jagged edges were slightly whitish where the metal had torn.

I'd like to say I still have the teaspoon, but I don't. I wasn't in the habit of keeping things in those days. Keeping something was a recognition that there would be a time in the future when you could look at an object and say, 'Oh yes, I remember that', or, 'Oh, that's when so-and-so happened', but as far as I was concerned, there would be no such time.

In the living room the television was still on, and the Norman Wisdom film hadn't yet ended.

•

Strange to say, there was a sequel to this terrible experience – or perhaps I shouldn't describe it as terrible? After all, the world was not, in the event, destroyed. Of course, it would truly have merited the name terrible if the world *had* been destroyed.

At any rate, I decided to write a letter to my MP.

I cannot now recall the exact words of the letter, since I wrote it twenty-eight years ago and didn't keep a copy; but I remember it pointed out that unannounced tests of this kind could cause a great deal of worry and anxiety. I posted it and expected to hear no more about it.

A few days later a pair of uniformed officers turned up at the door.

I asked them to come into the dining room and they sat down in the two chairs where I and my mother usually sat when we were having dinner. They were both very large men. One was large in every sense: fat and tall, with beefy forearms and a thick neck. He was sitting where I usually sat at dinner. He seemed barely to fit into the chair. The other was thin and tall, with a long sharp nose and fair hair. In fact, his hair seemed a little long for a policeman. He was sitting where my mother usually sat. It was very odd to see them there. Unbeknownst to them, I was sitting where my father usually sat.

The beefy one took out a folder, from which he carefully withdrew my letter. He handed it to me.

'You wrote this letter?' he asked me.

I took it. It was very odd to be receiving from him a letter I had written, and which I hadn't intended for the police, but for my MP.

'Yes,' I said.

'You're complaining about the siren.'

The use of the word 'complaining' was all too bald. I felt very hot under the collar. But I *had* been complaining about the siren. What else could you call it? The letter was indeed a fully-fledged complaint, not some general remarks about this and that. I didn't know quite how to reply, therefore. But to my surprise the fair-haired one came to my rescue.

'It certainly looks like it put the wind up you,' he said with a smile.

'Yes,' I said. 'I should think a lot of people were worried by it.'

'Unfortunately,' the beefy one said, unsmiling, 'we have to test the siren now and again to see if it works.'

This also – like his previous comment – seemed quite reasonable, and yet at the same time so unsympathetic that once again I didn't know quite what to say. The beefy policeman took the letter back from me without asking. This too seemed somehow odd: first he had given me my own property, which I had, as it were, ceded to another, viz., my MP; and now he was taking my own property back from me without asking, as if it were his. It seemed that nothing, when it came to the letter, was to my advantage.

'I understand that,' I said, 'but why didn't you tell anybody?'

'There's no requirement that we tell anybody,' said the beefy policeman.

'Why not?' I asked.

'Because there's no reason to,' he said.

'Why not?' I asked again, rather ashamed of myself that I had asked the same question twice, like a child.

'Because weren't in any danger.'

'But – how were we supposed to know that?' I asked, quite desperately.

The fair-haired one broke in, again smiling. 'If there's any danger,' he said, 'the public will be made aware beforehand.'

I must have looked puzzled by this, because the fair-haired one went on: 'The siren is for warning the public about any sort of threat. It may be floods, for example. In your letter you mention a nuclear attack. If there was any possibility of that there'd be a period of international tension first.'

'Would there?' I asked, not sure whether I intended the question to be satirical.

'Yes,' the fair-haired one said simply. 'There'd be a period – a couple of weeks or so – in which we might come to expect something like that. The public would be informed. If the siren went off during this period of international tension then it might mean there was an attack of the kind you mention.'

The beefy one looked at me. 'So there's nothing to worry about,' he said.

'How do you know there'd be a two-week period?' I blurted out.

The beefy one leaned forward very slightly. His belly was now on my letter. 'If you think about it,' he said, 'it stands to reason. There'd have to be a build-up of tension first. You'd read about it in the newspapers. Everyone would know about it.'

To me, this seemed almost a vision of paradise. I admit, girls, that I was even a little beguiled by it, that is, their notion that the end of the world would come not just at any time, but at the proper time, and after due warning and consideration.

The beefy one sat back into his chair. My letter ruffled up slightly at the passage of his body.

What happened next was quite confused. I stood up at the little dining table. I think I was hoping to end the interview at that point. I couldn't see any other way to end it, so I simply stood up. Unfortunately I knocked over a cup and saucer on the table, spilling cold tea everywhere. The policemen looked at the tea, as did I: no one made a move to do anything. The policemen obviously couldn't rush around helping, since it wasn't their house. Neither did I make a move to clear up the mess. The stream of tea ran right across the table, only stopping when it came to the beefy policeman's paperwork. The mishap, however, did not discourage me, as you might expect. On the contrary, girls, I felt somehow emboldened by it.

'I don't really feel,' I said, regarding them from my father's place at the table – or just above it – 'I don't really feel… that you're right about that. However, I understand what you have said. Thank you for coming.'

After a long pause the policemen now themselves got up. Perhaps they were unable to bear my position of authority above them. Both still had their eyes on the tea.

I ushered them out through the dining room door and into the hall. We all seemed to be walking as if in a dream. I opened the front door for the policemen, and they seemed to hesitate. They obviously felt that something further should be said. They hadn't managed to convince me on the matter of the siren. Because of the tea incident, they had somehow lost the thread.

Finally the beefy one managed something. 'As I say, it's a routine test. There's no need to worry.'

I, however, said nothing. I merely smiled in a way that let him know that I retained the right to disagree and disapprove, and closed the door on them.

After the policemen had left, I first went to clear up the tea, and then climbed the stairs to my room, where I lay on the bed. I wondered if I had truly asserted myself, and whether the small victory I had achieved had not been cancelled out by the ignominy of spilling the tea – not to mention by my failure, in fact, to advance any firm counter-argument of any kind.

We've started again. I suppose it must be approaching three o'clock in the morning. Why we needed to spend all that time at Durham bus station at this hour is beyond me.

I FEEL I ought to tell you girls just a little more about the chambermaid's daughter, because what happened after the encounter I have described – the second occasion, when I bumped into her just as I was leaving my room – was really quite funny. What happened was that as she brushed past me on her way into my room, she looked at me coquettishly, as I have said, and then she actually did say something, which was this: 'You want help.' She then entered my room. The door, which must have been a fire door, closed automatically behind her, leaving me standing alone in the empty corridor.

It was lunchtime, and I had planned to go downstairs to get some lunch. But now I felt unable to move from outside the door. I stood for a while, hesitating, my heart beating painfully. Finally, unable to think of anything else to do, I slowly walked away, to the end of the corridor, towards the stairs. But then I stopped again. What had she meant by saying 'You want help'? Was it in fact a statement or a question? Was it 'Do you want help?' or perhaps 'Do you want *to* help?' – that is, in making the bed? Was it, in fact, an invitation to help her? Had she in fact even said it at all, or had I imagined it? I actually toyed with this as a possibility, I think. Her words could have been some sort of hallucination. But no, I was sure that she had said *something*. I felt the urgent need to go back to her room – I should say, *my* room – to ask her what she had meant, though I couldn't think how I could phrase any question. Could

I say, for example, 'What did you mean by saying "you want help"?' Or would be a little weak? But, apart from that, I couldn't think what I *could* say. Nor could I think of a single excuse for going back to my room. She knew that I was on my way down for lunch.

Still, something wouldn't let me go down the stairs. So, slowly – very slowly – I retraced my steps. In the twinkling of an eye I found myself outside my own door. I still had no idea what I would say if I went back in. I put my ear nearer the door and listened. All was quiet. No sound of her footsteps nor of sheets being taken off. Nothing. This all seemed very odd. Surely I would have been able to hear something if she was making up the bed? Was she sitting down? Could it be that she was waiting for me to return? And so, if I did open the door, would she laugh at me, for doing something that she knew I would do? Would I go in there and see her all ready, in a chair, for my return, and hear her laugh? My hand closed around the doorknob, then relaxed, then closed around it once more. All of a sudden, I have no idea from where, I found the resolution to turn the knob. I pushed open the door.

She was not there.

I should say that it would have been impossible for her to have hidden in that tiny room. Every nook and cranny of the room was clearly visible from the door. The bed was at the far end, to the left; the sink was to the right. Sunlight streamed through the window from the deer park. The only other furniture was a small desk and wardrobe. The room was entirely empty – unpopulated. The bed hadn't been made up and there was no sign that anyone had been in there since I had left it.

It was impossible. Had she left quickly as I walked

away from her? My back was turned on her for perhaps twenty seconds. Could she have come out and disappeared somewhere else, in that time? And yet – I looked behind me – her trolley was still in the corridor. Had she gone into one of the other rooms in the corridor? Surely not!

Slowly, reluctantly, and feeling a sense of burning shame, I stepped backwards into the corridor, releasing my grip on the knob and letting the door close, and walked very slowly back the way I had come. I was utterly baffled, and, without really knowing why, quite mortified. I went down to lunch, but I had lost my appetite.

After a while, I forgot about it.

It was a couple of days after that, I think, that the chambermaid – the mother, I mean – asked me if I would like to go out with her daughter. I said no, as I have mentioned. After that, I don't remember seeing the chambermaid's daughter again.

Many years later – I can't remember when – I found myself thinking about this queer little episode, running it over in my mind. And as I did so – many years had passed – I realised the solution to the mystery. Strange that a gap of several years was necessary for me to find the solution.

She had been hiding in the wardrobe.

Yes, in the wardrobe. The clever little minx! For some reason it had never occurred to me that anyone would do such a thing. But it is the only explanation.

I have often felt that it should somehow be possible to rectify such a simple mistake. It should somehow be possible for me, now I know where she was, to walk into the room and throw open the doors of the wardrobe.

If she is still alive, I suppose that the chambermaid's daughter is now about forty-six. A little older, perhaps, than her own mother was at the time. Who knows how life has turned out for her? Perhaps she returned to Italy. Perhaps she went to university and trained to be a lawyer. Anything could have happened. It would certainly be wrong of me to assume that she followed her mother in her profession. This reminds me of a story I heard about an author whose name I have forgotten. During the Second World War this author was in London during the Blitz. The street he was living in was bombed, and one morning he woke to see a dreadful sight – some people were pulling a dead baby from the ruins of a house. The incident haunted him, and he later wrote a book about what might have happened to that baby had it lived, and about the great and good life that had been wasted. The book was an enormous success. The public responded strongly to the central idea – the pathos of that baby's unlived life, and the greatness it might have achieved. But it so happened that one of his readers was a man who lived in Sheffield. This man wrote to the author and told him that he had been born in that very street in London; that he had lived in that very house; and in fact that he *was* that baby. He had merely been unconscious when pulled from the rubble. He had moved to Sheffield and become a bus inspector.

I'm not sure quite how this applies to the chambermaid's daughter, but it proves, surely, that it is a mistake to assume too much.

The chambermaid's daughter was very attractive, so perhaps she didn't follow her mother in her profession, and instead had a remarkable career. Perhaps she became a model. If I went back to St Osyth's, perhaps I would be able to find out. Would her mother still be working there, at an advanced age? If not, would there be people working there who would remember her, and her daughter? Would St Osyth's be demolished? Would the deer park be covered in concrete? If not, and if the mother was still there, might her daughter be there with her, still? Is this utterly inconceivable? After all, the simplest thing that can happen is for things to stay the same. If I went back and found the daughter there, what would I tell her? Would we be able to laugh about it? We would certainly be older and wiser. Perhaps I would persuade her to go back to that room and get back into that wardrobe.

That is rather absurd.

Or perhaps, even after all this time, I would still not be able to talk to the chambermaid's daughter. Perhaps I would still be tongue-tied. Perhaps, too, if I did tell her it was me, and recounted what had happened, she would simply have forgotten it. Perhaps she would have had many lovers – her mother would have seen to that – and perhaps this single event, characterized, as it was, by nothing, rather than something happening, would not be very memorable to her after all these years.

Or perhaps she *would* remember it. Perhaps she would find it hard to forgive me for that day. I would see a sneer on her face, perhaps. Perhaps she would turn her back on me with contempt, even hatred. Perhaps my coming back after all these years to find her, aged forty-six and still a chambermaid, would be unbearable for her, and I would see in her eyes, not merely contempt and hatred, but terrible, terrible pain for all the wasted years.

•

I will almost certainly take that passage out. That's a bit much, I think. This memoir is gloomy enough without inventing things. For all I know the chambermaid's daughter is happy and successful, with a loving husband and lots of children. I don't feel I wronged her – why should I feel that? And I doubt if she feels wronged by me. I expect she is surrounded by orange trees and has her own swimming pool. I expect she has aged very well. I am sure – pardon the pun – that everything has gone swimmingly for her. Perhaps she has a little farm and grows cork. Even if she is still a chambermaid I have no reason to think that she is anything other than very happy.

Newcastle – though we didn't stop.

I FINALLY returned to Hull in the February of 1982, after having spent a month a St Osyth's. I had made a good recovery.

I found I was keeping up with my Chinese habit. The language soothed me, I think. I particularly enjoyed becoming more proficient in the writing system. I didn't know then, of course, that it would lead to the founding of the Institute.

.

I ought to say something briefly here about Hull itself. You are too young, girls, to know much of Hull, the city of your birth. Perhaps you would care to know why, in such unpromising circumstances, I decided to make it my home. Well, I have always found it to be a very pleasant place to live. The university, for example, is very well designed. It has a wonderful library, on seven floors, and in the 1980s, of course – the first half of that decade, at least – it was under the head librarianship of the poet Philip Larkin.

The environs of Hull are very attractive. For example, Hull has many sweeping crescent avenues where it is pleasant to stroll in the evenings. These avenues are notable for their cherry trees, gorgeous with blossom in spring. Hull also has many fine old parks, and its city centre has all that a busy metropolis can offer.

Nevertheless Hull is widely despised. It is hard to say why this is. Perhaps it is due to the fact that it has no outstanding building or monument of any kind, or that it is generally flat and low in aspect; or that many of its buildings and houses seem to be in a state of poor repair; or that there is a deal of waste ground; or that the population seem (if you fail to appreciate their good side) a little depressed and unfriendly; or that it is prone to disastrous floods; or that the climate is, in general, rather bleak; and that there is often a strange smell in the air; and so on. But I never felt that these things were in the least important.

As an example of the character of Hull, girls, let me describe an experience I had in a launderette, shortly after arriving.

It was late at night and I was sitting in the launderette, on Littlefair Street, waiting for an eiderdown to dry. The only other person in the launderette was an old woman who was slowly mopping the floor. She seemed very old indeed, and she was mopping in the slowest, most dispirited way imaginable. She was very thin, and her face was heavily wrinkled; quite terribly wrinkled, in fact. A cigarette bobbed at her mouth. (Those were the days when it was permissible to smoke anywhere, girls, even in a restaurant while others were dining, or in a swimming pool.) Then, all of a sudden, I heard a thud. I looked around, and saw that the old woman had fallen against one of the washing machines. Her body was slumped on the floor, and the top of her head was resting inside the concave glass door of the machine. I rushed over to her and bent down. The old woman's eyes were closed.

'Shall I get a doctor?' I shouted over the noise of the dryer. I put my lips closer to her ear and repeated the question. Still she didn't say anything. Finally I stood up and ran out of the launderette. The road outside was deserted. It was, I suppose, about eleven o'clock at night. There were no public houses in that area of town – except perhaps one or two of the type that no one goes in much, and whose only clientele consists of one or two old men sitting over a glass of beer, slowly rolling a cigarette and making munching movements with their jaws – and for a while I ran back and forth, looking for one of these pubs, or a shop, or anywhere with any sign of life. Nowhere was open. It was as if the launderette were the last island of light in Hull, and, now that the old woman had ceased pushing her mop, I was the only person left alive in Hull. There were not even any cars to flag down. So I continued running first one way, and then the other, fruitlessly. I knew that the old woman might be dying, and that it was my responsibility to do something about it, but this knowledge did nothing to help. After a couple more minutes I dashed back to the launderette to find the old woman in exactly the same position, slumped with her head resting inside the glass door. I shouted in her ear once more: 'Have you got a phone here?' She remained silent. The cigarette was still attached to her lower lip. With a sudden inspiration I ran to the back of the launderette, through a door marked 'Private': and there, as it had been all along, was a phone. I dialled for an ambulance and gave the name of the street and the launderette. Then I went back to the old woman. Her cigarette was still burning, drooping a great tip of ash. I bent down and tore it softly from her lip. 'They're coming,' I said, close to her ear. Her hair had a faint chemical scent. 'I've called an ambulance.' Close as I was, I now had the opportunity to examine her face. Something horrible had happened to it, I'm afraid. The skin had fallen in masses to the jaw and was hanging there: it was so wrinkled as to be almost corrugated. The eyes had heavy pouches. I took her hand. As I did so she opened her eyes and looked at me. It was very startling. The eyes were as vivid and unclouded as those of a young girl. I couldn't think why I hadn't noticed them before.

'There are tribes in Africa who use wooden blocks as a pillow,' I said to her, 'and you have chosen a glass door.'

Not long afterwards the ambulance arrived. The two men took her from the floor and placed her on a stretcher. She and I continued holding hands. Then we walked, the four of us, to the ambulance. At the moment of loading the stretcher into the back of the ambulance, my hand became detached from hers, and at that moment, in a harsh voice, she uttered a single word:

'Ellie.'

Then the ambulance-men closed the doors and drove off.

After my eiderdown had dried, I left, shutting the door behind me. The launderette was still lit up.

I REALISE that the foregoing anecdote doesn't really explain anything about the character of Hull – in any way.

Or does it? Perhaps the incident says more about Hull than I think it does. It's possible.

Certainly any rehearsal of the city's vital statistics, its imports, exports, what colour the telephone boxes are, and so on, would be useless in any attempt to elucidate the city's *soul*. And I have nothing else to offer, I'm afraid. What else can one offer, apart from one's own personal experiences?

However, there is one specific fact concerning Hull that I would like to mention. It isn't exactly a statistic, nor even really a fact: call it an impression. I mean the odour of Hull. It's very difficult to describe. It isn't exactly unpleasant, but then again neither is it pleasant. It's certainly not an organic odour. It doesn't smell as if it might originate from farming or fishing: occasionally farming smells do indeed drift over Hull, as they do over any city when the wind is in the right direction; and Hull, of course, is a port, and much connected with fishing, whaling, and so on, and so the smell of the sea and of rotting things very often settles over the city. But these are quite identifiable, and don't last very long – just until the wind changes. The real, native smell of Hull is something entirely different. What sort of a smell it is, it is difficult to say. It might come from an industrial process of some kind, but it doesn't smell like any chemical I am familiar with. It isn't the smell of paint, nor the volatile odour of spirits – nor the reek of insecticide. The nearest I could come to it would be to say it smells of *illness*. That, I realise, is a highly metaphorical way of describing something such as an odour, but then again, odours are very elusive things to describe. Do you know, girls, the smell that a sick-room sometimes takes on, when the bedclothes have been unchanged for days or weeks, when the room has been shuttered and filled with the exhalations of a sick person? When, if you are that sick person, your nose is full of horrible stuff and your tongue is furry and you haven't washed, and you are shut up in that room? *That* smell? Pervasive, cloying, as much a thing of the mind as a thing of the senses? That is the closest I could come to describing it. But of course this is entirely inadequate, as it fails to explain the origin of this peculiar odour. I became quite preoccupied by it when I first lived in Hull. I would ask people if they too had noticed it, and they would say: 'Oh yes, it's from the docks' or 'Yes, I've noticed that, what is it?' – but more often – and here is the astonishing thing, girls – they would look at me as if I were mad, and ask: 'What smell?' or 'No, I haven't noticed anything' – this when the stench was so bad you had to go out holding a handkerchief to your nose, and the smell came right into your house, and you could smell it in the bathroom with the hot tap turned full on! They had simply got used to it, as one does to the noise of traffic, or the hum of a computer, and stopped registering it. But it is quite real. If one leaves Hull, the smell vanishes from one's nostrils. It is certainly never present in Beijing. And yet when one returns from outside Hull, as soon as one steps out of the car or the plane – sometimes even before – there it is again, that odd, insidious, non-organic smell, the smell of mild illness. I can smell it now, describing it! The strange, unearthly odour of Hull!

As above.

Apropos OF Philip Larkin, I met the man himself on more than one occasion. The first time was in my fresher's week at the university. To describe this as a meeting is perhaps inaccurate. He came into the reference section on the ground floor of the library, where I was sitting, and said to me: 'Please don't eat in the library.'

There is something about libraries that excites me. What that is, I have no idea. Is it just the fact that a library is an extraordinary place? After all, so many voices are gathered there, in the one building: voices from all lands and times, a great confluence of voices. Yet some people treat a library as if it were just a big dump of mouldering books. A place for boredom, sullen silence and obedience, like a school. But I don't share that attitude. I become quite perceptibly excited as soon as I walk into a library. What is it that sets my skin prickling? The sheer beauty of books? The smell of them? I remember the first time I walked into the British Library in London and was confronted by the great display of golden spines that stands in the upper atrium. I stood before them and wept. So many brief, intense lives, blazing out; so much extraordinary labour and dedication.

In fact I could easily begin a subgroup of reminiscences based entirely on strange things that have happened to me in libraries. I will share just one with you, girls, before returning to the topic at hand. It was in the public library in Hull, about five years ago. The public library, I should stress, not the university library. All was peace and quiet – I was reading a book to make some notes for something that Guy wanted me to do – when all of a sudden a little man burst through the doors and began talking to one of the librarians at the desk. He was a fussy little man, brimming with energy and confidence. I think he was wearing a bow tie. It soon became clear that he was some sort of administrator or senior official at the library – perhaps even some sort of county official, with responsibility for several libraries. And it seemed he was quite well liked, too: the staff at the desk were all smiling. They all perked up and listened attentively to what he was saying. He was speaking in a really terrifically loud voice, as if he were addressing a hall full of people. Certainly everyone in the reading area – there were about ten of us – could hear every word, quite clearly: he was making no effort whatever – none at all – to hush his tone of voice. 'I think it'll all be finished by September,' he was saying. He had evidently just done something or achieved something that everyone had been hoping for, waiting and wishing for, something extremely important in their scheme of things, and the staff were all extremely pleased to hear the news. They were all smiling broadly and uttering little cries of congratulation. The little man continued talking – loudly talking over them in fact – his words really ringing out, laughing merrily, gesticulating, obviously enormously pleased with himself...

All of a sudden I stood up.

'EXCUSE ME I WOULD LIKE TO BORROW THIS BOOK!' I screamed at the top of my lungs.

Dead silence fell.

The desk staff seemed almost as flies trapped in

amber. So did the little man. A feeling of immense power was welling within me.

I walked quite leisurely up to the little man. I held up the book I was reading. 'I AM TRYING TO READ I HOPE YOU DON'T MIND THANK YOU VERY MUCH!' I shouted, quite insane with exultation.

Then I turned on my heel, without looking at any of them, and walked back to my seat. I buried myself once more in my book.

The scene at the desk was one of devastation. The little man was aghast. All the stuffing had been knocked out of him. The librarians were speechless, motionless, the smiles wiped from their faces. No one knew how to proceed; no one could even look at anyone else. What had been an occasion of joy had been turned, in a split second, into one of horror. I had dealt the little man a mortal blow, and in front of his troops, too, his workers; and they, the workers, guardians of the peace, had had their profession impugned, had been most egregiously insulted. Moreover I was clearly out of my mind. How to deal with me? How to go on? How to pick themselves up?

They remained like that for several seconds. The little man was the first to recover. 'Quite right, quite right,' he muttered. I raised a stealthy eye. The librarians were still in shock, unable to reply, still unable to look at each other. 'Quite right.' The little man made a few more comments *sotto voce*, and then slipped out. Silence descended once more, thickly.

After about five minutes I too left. I had decided against borrowing the book. I went home. All the madness had drained away, and I actually found it quite hard to remember why I had done it.

As above.

UNFORTUNATELY I'M always doing things like that. Of course, the little man was annoying, but there were lots of other ways I could have dealt with him. For example, I could have gone up to him and said in a soft voice, 'Excuse me – do you mind if I have a word? I think you are talking rather loudly. Would you mind keeping it down?' Or, even more politely, 'I'm sorry to bother you, but as I'm sure you'll appreciate, this is a library, and we are trying to read. If it wouldn't be too much trouble, I'd be grateful if...' – although that is perhaps *too* polite. That might even sound sarcastic.

However, a happy medium *could* have been struck. And so, instead of the terrible destruction I had wreaked, a friendly atmosphere could have been preserved. The desk staff would have looked on, perhaps a little surprised at first to see their superior upbraided, but conscious that I was in the right, and ready to forgive me. The little man would have been entirely won over. He would have apologized profusely, and, on his way out, would perhaps have come over to me again as I sat in my chair. 'I just wanted to say... thank you for pointing that out,' he might have said. 'I really don't know what came over me... You were right, of course...' And from then on we would have been friends, and I would occasionally even have seen him in town where he would have given me a cheery wave or a smile...

Oh God, what nonsense.

I just don't seem to improve with age. Even quite recently I did the most shockingly insensitive thing. It was about ten months ago – just before last Christmas, in fact. I was reading a free newspaper in the television room. On the letters page, one of the readers had written in to say that she had always loved Christmas time, and loved especially the story of Jesus' birth in the stable, where he had been laid in a manger because there was no room at the inn. This reader found it remarkable that three kings had travelled all the way from the East, led by a star. The editor had bestowed on it the distinction of 'star letter' – perhaps as a joke, since it was concerned in part with the 'star' of Bethlehem – and had enclosed it in a red box.

For some reason the letter infuriated me. Among all the shoddy advertisements and sham articles about local businesses it seemed the crowning piece of provincial idiocy and ignorance. In the flush of my contempt I composed a reply. 'Dear Madam,' I began, 'The story of Jesus' birth is a myth. There never was any birth in a stable. In fact there is no mention of a stable in the New Testament. Jesus was probably born in October. These stories from a two thousand-year-old Jewish tradition cannot serve us in the twenty-first century. I recommend that you discard them, Sincerely, etc.' I put my name and address at the top, and addressed the envelope to the woman: the newspaper, surprisingly, had seen fit to print her full address. Afire with missionary zeal, I put the letter in the postbox in the hall. I was proud of the fact that I had put my own name and address at the top of the letter. I wasn't hiding from this woman, after all. I wished to stand up and be counted.

However, soon afterwards – probably the following day – I began to wonder whether it had been such a good idea. Might there be unforeseen consequences? I felt, as I had in the library, a strong sense of deflation. Was my response not perhaps a little excessive? Need I even have responded at all? Why not let the woman – perhaps it was an old woman – continue with her simple faith, to the end? Why destroy it? It would certainly be a comfort to her on her deathbed to have in mind the image of the radiant Christ-child on his bed of straw, offering up in his person the sure and certain hope of resurrection. Why was I so arrogant? Did I know all the answers? And what about that detail of the 'Jewish' tradition? Now I came to think of it, that could easily be misinterpreted. I had simply meant to point out that the story of the nativity originated from a culture far removed from our own, in time as well as in space, and that we had simply adopted it – the fact that it was 'Jewish' was neither here nor there. My thoughtless words now seemed to have a somewhat sinister ring. Was there some slight suggestion of antisemitism? No! No! That was certainly not what I meant! I simply wanted... But now I looked at it, the whole letter, in all its aspects, seemed extraordinarily ill-advised. I wasn't actually sure, for example, that Jesus *had* been born in October. I'd merely heard it somewhere. Add to that the possible repercussions for the woman, which could be very severe, even life-threatening... What if she were ill, for example, and because of my letter went into a rapid decline? That would almost be murder! And what would the relatives do? The woman would show them the letter, holding it out to them with trembling hands, with my address on top! *Ecce homo...* Oh, God! How stupid to have included my address! The relatives would know exactly where to find me! I was an idiot!

But the relatives never did come to find me, I'm glad to say.

Still somewhere on the A1. I should really get some sleep.

NEITHER DOES the second occasion on which I met Larkin really deserve the name of a meeting. It was one Saturday morning, at Chester's, the bakery in Sallowpool. Larkin was in there buying a French loaf. I saw him through the window as I came past, and recognized him immediately. I was surprised, because a French loaf was the last sort of bread one would imagine Larkin might buy.

As it happened I was in a rather strange mood. I had just had an encounter with a two tramps. I could go on at length about these tramps, since there is rather a long story connected with them – they had stolen some money from me a week earlier – but this is probably not the place to go into it. I had just that moment, before seeing Larkin, been involved in an argument with one of these tramps, which had ended with me walking away and poking out my tongue, I'm sorry to say – it sounds horrible, girls, but there had been the provocation of the theft – to which the tramp in question had responded with a torrent of abuse in which the words 'I'm going to cut your tongue out' were prominent. So I was in a rather strange mood, and when I passed Chester's, and saw Larkin through the plate-glass window buying the French loaf, I decided to go in, just to see what might come of it. I had no plan in mind – none at all – but thought, I suppose, that I would find the courage to say something to him. I had always admired Larkin's poetry, and wanted to find some way of telling him so. Or perhaps, to be honest, I just wanted to wring some sort of word from him. I was curious about him. So I pushed the door open smartly. Unfortunately, however, Larkin chose just that moment to turn from the counter towards the door, holding the bread out, with the result that I hit his loaf with the edge of the door. Chester's is a small bakery and rather cramped. The bread wasn't at all damaged; it didn't break, or even bend. It was just a minor collision, a tiny knock. Larkin looked at me and said 'sorry' in a deep voice. He seemed mildly annoyed. Simultaneously I too said 'sorry'. That was a golden opportunity, I knew it even at the time: the ice had been broken. We had actually exchanged words. Here, now, then, was my chance. But how to continue a conversation with someone whose French loaf you have only nearly, but not quite damaged? If I had damaged it properly, I could have offered to pay for a new one, and then anything might have come of it. But merely bumping lightly into the loaf, at most knocking a flake or two of crust off, was not enough to merit more than the 'sorry' I'd already tendered. To start a conversation now would have required some very adroit manoeuvre, and unfortunately I couldn't think of any such manoeuvre. And while such thoughts were going through my mind – very rapidly and incoherently, the way such thoughts do – Larkin brushed past me and left the shop. I was still holding the door open. And at that moment the assistant asked me what I wanted. She didn't even wait for me to go to the counter. So I now had to attend to my own purchase, and the whole thing had been a failure. At the same time, because of the encounter with the tramp, my mind was still running along strange channels. As a consequence I said the very first thing that came into my mind, which surprised even me. It was this: 'Do you have any frog bread?'

The assistant looked at me narrowly and asked me to repeat the question.

I did so.

'Do you mean French bread?' she asked. She was a middle-aged woman with a severe expression. She was obviously long used to dealing with students and other troublemakers.

'No, no,' I said, attempting a casual laugh, 'Frog bread.' I hoped, I think, that she would take it as a reference to some very obscure type of bread, perhaps from a far-flung region of the world, such as the Middle East. It was essential that the bakery wouldn't have what I asked for, since I didn't have a single penny on me. I glanced out of the window. To my astonishment Larkin was still there, outside, gazing in at me through the window. It gave me quite a shock. He was like a bluebottle that you think has flown off, but which, when you look, you find has settled on your hand. Then, as I watched, another figure joined him: a small woman with a thick felt coat and hair that had recently been in curlers. Larkin turned away from the window to talk to her.

'I've worked here for fifteen years,' the woman persisted, 'and I've never heard of "frog bread". What sort of bread is it?'

'It's a medieval bread,' I said, again utterly astonished at my own words.

For some reason that seemed to satisfy the woman. 'No,' she said. 'You'll have to make it yourself.'

'Thank you,' I said. I left the bakery. Larkin and his friend were still outside, talking. I heard a snatch of their talk as I passed: they were discussing where else they needed to go and what they needed to buy. There was no hope of my interrupting them; and besides, I still couldn't think of anything to say.

The coach has just stopped.

THE DRIVER has pulled in at the side of the carriageway. What is he doing? He's leaving the coach... That's strange... Ah, yes, I see. They really should supply these coaches with toilets. Especially for the girls.

Everyone else is asleep. I can see Guy, up at the front, her head illuminated by the driver's cockpit light, doubtless dreaming about the forthcoming demonstration; Tim, his head still lolling to the side; near me is the Chinese girl, huddled into a coat; behind is 'Beaver'. I am the only person awake, apart from the driver, of course. I have my little overhead light on so I can continue to scribble. The rest of the coach is in darkness.

Ah, the driver is getting back on. Guy stirs slightly as the engine starts up. The driver pulls out onto the empty carriageway, bearing his cargo of sleeping girls.

The driver is in rather an odd position. He doesn't share any of our goals and ideals: he is merely a paid servant. Yet while we snooze, he carries the responsibility for the success of the entire enterprise.

The way he hunches over his steering wheel is suggestive: he looks as if he is running his fingers around the lip of a cauldron. He is about my age, I suppose. Should I go and speak to him? Perhaps he would welcome the company.

•

I will go in a moment.

As above.

THE THIRD occasion on which I met Philip Larkin was very late at night. It was perhaps two o'clock in the morning. I was walking aimlessly into the university campus.

From Cottingham Road there is a long, wide path, ungated, bordered by shrubs and lawns, that leads into the heart of the university. At the far end of the path is the library block. I would guess that this path is two hundred and fifty yards long, and it is quite straight. I had just started out on it, coming from the road, when I noticed, at the far end – two hundred and fifty yards off – a tiny figure emerging from the library. Such a thing was somewhat unusual at that time of night, since of course the library had shut several hours ago.

The figure began to walk towards me, towards the main road. It and I were the only two human souls on the campus. If we continued on our present courses our paths would cross.

Two hundred and fifty yards is quite a long way for two persons to walk towards each other, knowing that they will pass each other in the middle. There is a sense of anticipation, especially if it is two o'clock in the morning and no one else is around. However, there was nothing else for it, since the path had no turning-off-point and only one major intersection, a covered walkway right in the middle, at the hundred and twenty-five yard mark.

After perhaps fifteen paces (during which of course the figure had progressed fifteen of his own paces), I had a better view of him. At this point I began to suspect it was Philip Larkin. In fact, I think even at the very beginning I suspected it was Larkin, because who else could have emerged from the library at two o'clock in the morning? Only a member of staff could do that, and most of the other members of staff were female. This figure, it was obvious, was not female. And when we had about a hundred and fifty yards between us, I was certain it was Larkin. Larkin was quite recognizable, even at this distance: tall, bald, soberly clad, with black-framed spectacles, exactly as he had looked outside Chester's – exactly as he always looked, in fact, rain or shine. I thus had a hundred and fifty yards in which to decide what to say to him.

Here, girls, was my third chance to say something to Larkin – about his poetry, or indeed about anything else. But I could think of nothing appropriate to say in the middle of the night, in a deserted university. I racked my brains. Larkin was getting nearer, nearer to the crossways, and was perhaps himself beginning rather to wonder about me. He might, I thought, be almost as uneasy as I, because the long build-up was wearing on the nerves. Perhaps he suspected that I had recognized him, and was bracing himself for whatever I might say. Perhaps he was even imagining me desperately trying to think of something to say. He didn't recognize me, obviously, since the encounter in Chester's, and before that, in the library, had been utterly unexceptional.

I could now hear his footfalls, as he could doubtless hear mine. Whatever I said would have to be pretty good, because I'd had a great deal of time to think about it. In the bakery I'd had to act on the spur of the moment, to rely on my wits, which, in the event, were not very reliable: all I had managed was 'sorry'. In fact in almost any situation in which one might meet

Larkin, one would have to say something immediately to him, just like that, without any convenient time for reflection. If I were introduced to Larkin at a party, for example, I'd have to say something right away, such as: 'I'm very glad to meet you, sir; I have enjoyed reading your poetry,' which would be rather limp. But here I had almost a minute – though that time was now rapidly dwindling – to think of something worthy of the situation. But what, in fact, *did* the situation demand? If I said something witty, perhaps even quoted a line from his own verse, he'd know I'd had almost a minute to think of it, and this would be rather shaming, especially if it turned out not to be very witty or very good. I was caught in something of a quandary. If I said 'Hello Mr Larkin, I enjoy your poetry,' it would seem witless after two hundred and fifty yards; and yet if I said something complex, perhaps in honour of our nocturnal convergence, it would seem forced. But I had no time, now, to ponder these alternatives. Larkin was now quite near, and I hadn't thought of anything, neither a complex thing nor a simple thing, to say to him. And it certainly *was* Larkin, of that there was absolutely no doubt. I could even rule out the possibility that it was a very remarkable simulacrum of Larkin. A tall man, imposing, a suggestion of jowls, spectacles, wearing a dark overcoat, hurrying along, bald head down, tightly buttoned up, eager to get home, carefully scarved, carrying a dark leather briefcase – and, to top it off, having just emerged from the library. Impossible that it was anyone else. We were now twenty yards apart. Now fifteen. Our paths would meet precisely at the covered walkway. Ten yards: five. We both stepped under the covered walkway. Larkin was not looking at me. He was hurrying on. My mind was utterly empty. He was on me. He was right at my shoulder. I had a sudden intense impression of him: I smelled his coat.

'It's all go today,' I said loudly.

Larkin turned in mid-step and threw me a look. He didn't seem very surprised.

'Yes it is,' he rumbled, with a small nod of the head. He stepped off the covered walkway onto the other side, and kept going. Five yards, ten, twenty, footfalls receding. I couldn't help watching him as he walked away from me. I knew he would not turn again.

He was gone.

Goodbye, my darling!

As above.

LARKIN WROTE very eloquently about love, of course, and in one of his poems he says that love, having failed a woman in youth, could not help her as an old woman because she was too old. Unfortunately I can't remember the title or anything else in the poem. If I were at home I'd look it up.

The poem struck me forcibly when I first read it. I think I found myself in broad agreement with the poet. The woman had gone utterly beyond the reach of love. To be fair to Larkin, he was speaking of romantic love only. Other sorts of love, such as the love of children or of dogs, were presumably still available to her.

But then I read a poem by Yeats. Unfortunately I have forgotten the title of this poem as well and cannot quote a single word from it. I am afraid I am reliant entirely on my memory here on this coach, which, as you can see girls, isn't very good. I will certainly look it up when I get home. This poem presented a diametrically opposed view. Yeats suggested that old women *could* still love, and be loved; they *could* still be healed, wounded, destroyed, reborn by love, in precisely the same way as younger women could. Here, then, was a much more humane treatment of the subject. An old woman was not merely a piece of human detritus, fit for the scrap-heap.

Which of these poems was the truer? The Larkin position was certainly blunt. Love *could* not help her now. And after all, there is something to be said for this. For an old woman – such as Ellie, the one I'd seen sweeping the launderette – what possible hope could there be? Was a young man about to burst into the launderette and present her with a bunch of roses? Certainly no – never! How could anyone feel passion for Ellie? And what would romantic love really mean if it were devoid of passion? For Ellie, it *was* time to put away hopes of love – love between man and woman – and prepare for the inevitable. Even if a lover did present himself and went down on one knee, what could Ellie do? With daily cares, and a launderette to mop? With a husband in tow, perhaps a sick one?

And yet, to my mind, Larkin did not seem entirely to have won the argument. You will admit that his view is hardly balanced. He did not say that such and such a thing was the most likely outcome: he said, baldly, that it was the *only* outcome. And it was this, so to speak, super-confidence, I think, that gave Yeats the chink, as it were, to slip through and unravel everything. For despite the fact that we all know that love is often defeated, and that many people go to their graves unloved, and that most men are disinclined to fall in love with old women with sagging faces, these are not laws of life, but mere probabilities. And what is the essence of the human spirit – at any age – but defiance of probabilities? Defiance of death, defiance of age, defiance of infirmity? Laughing in the face of the inevitable? Love is not humble! Love proclaims: *I am.* Unbidden, love surges up in the human breast. Yes! Look on this aged body if you must; look at this corrugated skin. But then meet my gaze, and you will see, looking back, the eyes of a fourteen-year-old girl, tender, trusting, lively and full of joy.

As above.

Now I come to think of it, the old woman's name was not Ellie: she had simply *said* 'Ellie'. Ellie was presumably someone else.

I believe we just passed through Dunbar. It will be light soon.

But I have strayed a little from the chronological order of my story. I still haven't said how I became closer to Madeleine.

It happened like this.

After my time at St Osyth's, I returned to Hull, as I have said, in the February of 1982, to the house with Madeleine and Henry, as well as the other young man whose name I can't remember, and Lara (I'm not sure if I mentioned Lara: she lived on the top floor). I think the others were a bit surprised to see me. They had all but given me up for dead.

They had done nothing whatever to improve the appearance of the house. It was still the same – the same cold hallway, broken bulbs, and so on. The dinosaurs were still there. As soon as I got back I decided to make my room, at least, a little more comfortable. My parents had given me some money, and with it I bought a proper bed, as well as a new desk and chair. I also bought a plant, a new rug and a new heater, which I kept on almost constantly. I was determined not to get so ill again. I also painted out the diplodocus and put up some hanging scrolls. My parents were rather perplexed by my decision to continue living in Hull, I think. After all, I had left the university, so what point was there in living in a run-down old house with blown bulbs? Why go back to that? Especially in my rather weak condition? Yet that would be to fail to take into account the peculiar charms of Hull, and the people I had made friends with, and Madeleine herself.

I was still in love with Madeleine, of course. I began

thinking of ways I could get to speak to her. But unfortunately she never came out of her room. I didn't want simply to turn up at her door again. She did use the toilet, of course, but it was impossible to tell when she would do it – and it would have been embarrassing to accost her outside the toilet door.

I decided that the best way to proceed would simply be to write Madeleine a note inviting her to go for a walk with me. A note, I decided, would be less painful for both of us.

I spent some time thinking what I ought to write. Finally, after several drafts, I rejected the idea of a note altogether. Instead, I thought, I would draw a picture. That would be more original. Accordingly I drew a picture of myself sitting at my desk, with a speech bubble coming out of my mouth that said: 'The weather's so nice, I wonder if Madeleine would like to come for a walk in Swinewoods with me?' I drew myself as accurately as I could, coloured it in with some pencils and included some of the things in my room, most particularly my new plant. I was, as I have said, quite proficient at drawing: chiefly dinosaurs, but I could turn my hand to other subjects.

I put the drawing in an envelope, addressed it to Madeleine, and then went downstairs and slipped it under her door. As previously, I heard the noise of springs as Madeleine got out of bed. She must therefore have seen it come under the door. I hurried up the stairs on tiptoe.

I returned to my room and listened for any noise. Madeleine's door hadn't opened. There was only silence. It occurred to me that there might be someone else with Madeleine in her room: but since Madeleine's name was on the envelope, presumably they wouldn't open it. After waiting for ten minutes, I decided that Madeleine wasn't going to come out immediately, and so went down the stairs – noisily, this time – and into the kitchen, where Henry and the young man whose name I can't remember were chatting. I exchanged a few words with them. But as I did so, I felt a terrible jolt. I realised that I hadn't signed the note.

What a fool! I hadn't signed it! I had relied on Madeleine to be able to recognize me from my drawing of myself! It hadn't even occurred to me to sign it. After all, why would I sign a cartoon? But it was by no means certain that she would be able to see that it was me. It might be interpreted as being Henry, or even the young man whose name I can't remember. The fact that I had drawn the furniture in my room was of no help: Madeleine had never been into my room. The note simply read: 'The weather's so nice, I wonder if Madeleine would like to come for a walk in Swinewoods with me?'

Henry looked at me strangely: he could see that something odd was going on.

At that very moment I heard a sound. It was Madeleine's door opening and Madeleine herself coming into the hallway. Instead of standing my ground I'm afraid that I panicked. I ran into the bathroom. As soon as I'd slid the bolt home I heard Madeleine's boots coming into the kitchen.

'Did you draw this?' she asked the young man whose name I can't remember in forthright tones.

'No,' he replied.

'You?' she asked Henry.

'No,' Henry laughed.

There was a brief pause, and then the young man whose name I can't remember said something in a low voice that I couldn't quite hear.

'Oh,' Madeleine said when he had finished. She didn't sound particularly pleased. There was another pause. Then I heard her boots approaching the bathroom door. There were two loud knocks.

'No, I don't mind going for a walk in Swinewoods, Nicholas!' she called out.

Then I heard her leaving the kitchen.

When I came out of the bathroom Henry was holding the picture I had drawn Madeleine.

•

I wonder if the girls are at all perplexed by all this? After all, it doesn't have a great deal to do with them. It concerns a woman of whom they know nothing. Will they really want to read about how their father fell in love so many years ago, in a time before they were even born, with a woman they do not know, before they were even thought of? Will it not all be simply an embarrassing irrelevance?

I hope not. It all depends on what age they are when they read this. Of course, it isn't addressed to them as they are now. They are only young. Thirty or forty would be a good age, I think: or even later, when people can forgive almost anything. And it is inevitable that some time in the future they too will fall in love. Perhaps then the experiences of their father will be of some interest.

On reflection, I will have to hide this memoir from them quite carefully. But I have so many papers! When I think of my desk at home I feel hot all over. I will have to sort them out quite thoroughly before I die, to stop them falling into the wrong hands. And then there are these asides I've written… When will I take them out? Will I have time to take them out? What if I die in an accident? What if this coach crashes? Then I won't be able to edit my notes, my diaries, and so on. The girls will have them as they are, unreconstructed… In fact, I shouldn't even be writing this…

I must just say one thing about Henry, however. Both he and the young man whose name I can't remember seemed highly amused by my note to Madeleine. We were all very young, of course, and youth is a time when all sorts of destructive and painful experiments are carried out: nevertheless I could have wished for a little more sympathy on this occasion.

Henry in general showed remarkably little concern for other people's feelings. For example, he treated the teacher he was involved with – the one I have mentioned, with whom he had consummated a relationship on a train – very badly. She once came to Hull in a state of some distress. She turned up one afternoon at the house in Christiania Street, having travelled all the way up from London that morning: Henry wasn't in, and it was I who answered the door. I told her that Henry was at the university and would be back soon – this was shortly before he too dropped out of his course – and invited her in for a cup of tea. She accepted and came through into the little dining room with the painting of the iguanodon, a thin woman with curly reddish hair, carrying a russet handbag. I could see that she had been crying. She didn't seem to want to say much, and I began talking about my experience in the launderette with the old woman, which had occurred recently. She kept playing with the mug of tea I had given her, not really drinking it, clutching her handbag on her lap, unwilling or unable to respond; and I began to wonder what Henry would do when he came *home, and whether he would treat the situation with the sensitivity it deserved. You would have thought that a woman in her mid forties, a teacher, would have had more sense than to give up her job and her whole life, in fact, to pursue a teenager – which is essentially what Henry was – but I suppose there is no accounting for love, as indeed my reading of the poem by Yeats had led me to reflect. I was just about to leave the woman alone in the dining room – considering that she might perhaps prefer it – when I heard the door bang. Henry came into the dining room, accompanied by Madeleine.*

The teacher immediately rose from her chair, clutching her handbag in front of her.

'I wrote you a letter,' the woman said to Henry, looking at him with shining eyes – seemingly oblivious to the fact that Madeleine and myself were there in the room – 'and rather than post it I thought I'd come up and give it to you myself.'

This was obviously her little joke, which she now delivered in a rather breathless manner, having obviously prepared it some time in advance; perhaps days, or even weeks. She hadn't envisioned, I suppose, the present situation, i.e. that two other people would be in the room when she delivered the joke, but she was set on her course, and nothing could change it. She reached into her handbag, retrieved an envelope with the familiar spidery handwriting, and held it out to Henry. At this moment, however, a small disaster befell her. Overwrought as she was, a small drop of material shot from her nose and landed on the letter. The woman saw what had happened – indeed, we all saw it – but didn't attempt to wipe it off, preferring to pretend that this small drop of material didn't exist. Her hand, still holding out the letter, began to shake.

After what seemed an age, Henry reached out a hand and took the letter, contaminated as it was by this drop. As he took it, the woman began to shake all over.

What Henry then did was unforgivable, I think. He held the letter in front of him and tore it in half.

It was exactly as if he were tearing the woman.

She uttered a cry and started toward Henry, but Henry retreated a step, his face radiating cruelty, and tore the two halves of the letter into quarters. Then he threw the quarters onto the floor. The woman, sobbing, sank to her knees to retrieve the fragments; and then, in a spasm of despair, swept them violently aside, rose to her feet, pushed past us, ran down the corridor and out into the street, leaving the front door wide open.

Madeleine and I looked after her in astonishment. This woman was old enough to be our mother. What had Henry done to her?

As above.

I HOPE you will agree, girls, that in the last few hours we have come quite a long way. I hope I have given you a good picture of what life was like in Hull all those years ago, before you were born; and perhaps you are even beginning to understand what I am doing here, on this coach. Now I will tell you just a little of what happened when Madeleine and I went for our walk together in Swinewoods. After that we can get onto more important things, such as the circumstances of your birth.

Swinewoods is a low area of scrub and forest just to the north of Hull, up towards Beverley. I had been there many times for walks, and was always a little surprised to see how few other people were there. None of the university students seemed to know or care about it. And it was only a matter of a three-quarter-hour walk from the university! Such beauty, for the taking!

I arranged with Madeleine that we would go the next morning, which happened to be a Saturday. It worried me a little that she'd agreed to go so readily, and so soon. Did she simply want to get it out of the way, to discharge, as it were, her responsibilities, and then let the whole matter die a natural death? But there was nothing I could do about that. I was just glad she'd agreed. So, at about ten o'clock the following morning, I knocked on her door and we set off. We walked out of the town via the Ditch Bridge, and then took country roads for the mile or so to the woods. It was a beautiful day – spring had now begun in earnest – and the hedgerows were full of ramsons, which gave off their characteristic garlicky scent. Occasionally a horse trotted by. Madeleine seemed quite used to walking – I suppose it was her upbringing in Scotland – and we arrived at the woods in good time.

We began by talking about her studies. Madeleine was now nearing the end of her university course, and in fact would be graduating in June. It emerged that she wanted to work with people.

'Why?' I asked.

'Why not?' Madeleine replied, with a surprised look. 'I like people. I'd like to work with addicts.'

For some reason this saddened me a little.

'How about you?' Madeleine continued. 'You're not at the university any more, are you?'

'No.'

'Do you have any plans?'

'No.'

'Why not?'

'I don't know. It all seems pointless.'

'Why pointless?' Madeleine asked.

I stopped by a dead tree and ran my hands over the silvery wood. 'Do you really think we're all going to be here in a year's time?'

'Why shouldn't we be?' Madeleine replied. 'I intend to be.'

'Can you simply intend something, and have it come true?' I asked.

'Of course you can,' Madeleine said. 'Don't be stupid.'

I think at that point Madeleine's frankness – her rudeness, some might say – gave me the courage to speak. I will admit that the issue is something I feel strongly about. In fact it tends to override all other considerations. I find I have the ability to speak with great passion on this matter, when on other matters I might remain silent.

'Let me explain,' I said to Madeleine. 'When I go to bed at night, I think, before I go to sleep, of dying in the night. When I wake up I wonder if we'll get through the day. If I hear loud noises I imagine it's happened – the end of the world. I sit up in bed with my heart pounding. Sometimes I imagine noises. Or a flash of light. I sit up and listen, but I'm still alive. Sometimes in my dreams there are explosions, and I'm hiding, trying to get away, but I know I can't escape.'

I paused and looked at Madeleine's face. It wore the same indecipherable expression I had seen when I'd danced with her in the kitchen. This time I could see it from rather closer up.

'Of course, there's nothing we can do about it,' I continued, a little excited by the effect I was having on her. 'Nothing will stop it. It will happen soon, and then we'll all be dead. The whole earth, with all its animals and trees, our museums, our civilizations, our books and libraries, all gone, and we, the survivors, with nothing to eat but ash, all our friends and family gone, our loved ones, and no way back... a wasteland...' I gulped. 'Perhaps we are the only creatures in the universe that can think. And we'll just throw it all away, for nothing, because we're too stupid to live with one another. That's the sort of people we are. We don't deserve to live. Yes – we deserve everything we get. And that's why' – I said with a sudden inspiration – 'I have nothing to offer you.'

This was all rather immature, of course. But it had a magical effect on Madeleine. Continuing to gaze at me, she linked her arm with mine.

'That is so stupid,' she said.

I sometimes wonder what Madeleine would say if she could see me now. And what would she say about you two girls? Perhaps she has little girls of her own now. Would she be surprised to see the life I have made for myself? Perhaps she knows all about me – it's hard to be a private person these days. I'm sure she's looked me up on the internet. If so, she will have seen how I'm getting on, and will know all about the Institute. It sometimes seems amazing to me that after all the bad luck I had, and all the heartache, that things turned out as they did. I have more than once wished she would come along to the Institute. She would certainly be a lot older, but I don't think she would have changed a great deal. I know women can change very greatly from the ages of twenty to forty, but I have the feeling she would still be very attractive.

But this is actually just waffle. I really have no idea what Madeleine would look like.

After we had returned from our walk I thought a great deal about what had passed between us, and decided that, although she had linked her arm with mine, it was still unsatisfactory, from numerous points of view. First, I hadn't kissed her. Second, she hadn't laughed. Third, she let go my arm shortly afterwards. Fourth, we didn't make any plans to meet again.

It would have been rather odd, I suppose, to plan to meet again, seeing as we both lived in the same house.

I WILL admit to being quite nervous of coach travel. I keep thinking the coach is going to crash. I feel obscurely that I have to stay up to keep the driver awake.

I remember another coach journey I took many years ago. This would have been in the late 1970s or early 80s. Sitting across the aisle from me were two teenaged boys. These boys seemed pleasant enough – they weren't shouting or playing loud music or making a nuisance of themselves – but they had insisted on bringing a quantity of beer onto the coach. It was a hot summer's day. As the journey went on, they naturally began to wish to use a toilet. But unfortunately there were no toilet facilities on the coach, and we were on a long trip with no scheduled breaks. What they did was inventive, though rather anti-social. They...

Perhaps it's not really that bad. It pertains, after all, to bodily functions familiar to all children.

They used the empty beer-cans. Yes, girls, I'm afraid so. It was all done quite discreetly. I think I was the only person who knew what they were up to.

But then something unfortunate happened. Without realizing it, one of the boys – quite drunk – knocked over one or more of the cans – the ones they had used – and the contents ran down the length of the coach, past the feet of a good dozen passengers, finally forming a little pool at the back of the coach. And at the very back, on the brink of this pool, a grandmother was sitting with her young grandson.

This grandmother waited until the coach had reached its destination, and then, as she passed the boys on her way out, told them exactly what she thought of them. I won't say what she said.

The strange thing was, the boys looked very contrite when they heard her words. It was really quite heart-breaking, looking at them. They couldn't quite understand, it seemed, that what she was saying really applied to them.

Edinburgh. Everyone still asleep. This coach has taken an incredible amount of time to get here. I didn't think it would take this long. We've really gone around the houses.

A COUPLE of days after our walk I met Madeleine in the road in Christiania Street. I'd heard the door slam and thought it might be her going out to the corner shop; accordingly I waited a couple of minutes and followed her, knowing that I would probably meet her coming back with a pint of milk. Perhaps it was a little obvious, doing such a thing: but it worked like a charm. It was about nine o'clock at night, and the sun had long since set. In Hull the lamps light the sky on cloudy nights and turn the whole firmament orange, and so Madeleine was lit with a faint orange glow as she came towards me, made more orange by the fact that she was still wearing her orange dress. She was carrying a small loaf of orange bread.

'I'm just going for a walk,' I said. 'Would you like to come?'

'Where are you going?' Madeleine asked. 'I don't want to be back late.'

'Just to a place I know,' I replied.

To my surprise she agreed. I waited while she dropped off her orange loaf. I knew exactly where I could take her – a place known as the Quarry. I was fairly sure that she wouldn't know it, because the Quarry was not in fact open to the general public. It was for members only. The Quarry, I should explain, wasn't actually a quarry. It had once been a quarry, many years ago, but had been re-landscaped as a garden. It was in the grounds of a very expensive hotel –

also called the Quarry – and was for the use of the hotel guests. I, however, had discovered a way in through a gap in an iron railing. I often visited late at night, when no one was around. In my younger days, girls, I was not perhaps as law-abiding as I am now, but I certainly treated the Quarry with every respect.

I led Madeleine the half-mile or so to the Quarry and showed her the gap in the railing, on a bank about four feet above the pavement. At first Madeleine was a little reluctant to attempt the bank and then squeeze through the gap, but I told her that there was never anyone about in the garden, and that if we timed it right, no one would see – and in any case, once we were in, who was to know we weren't guests? After a while Madeleine agreed. I waited until the road was quiet, and then vaulted up on the bank first, to show her what to do: I put out my hand to help her, but Madeleine made it up easily on her own. We went over to the railings and I parted the ivy covering the gap – it was full of cobwebs, but that didn't bother me – and went through first. I put my hand back through the gap to encourage her to come after me. This time she took it, and I pulled her in. Her hand felt small and soft.

We came out amid a clump of trees and looked around us. The garden was shaped like a bowl, or better, a long scoop in the earth. At the front of the scoop was the hotel, a black mass in the darkness with one or two lit windows: at the back was a high slope accessible via a flight of stairs, with, at its base, an ornate fountain. A little bridge spanned the garden from side to side. Beneath our feet the grass was springy, and there was the warm smell of moist earth. The occasional star could be seen through the clouds.

After walking for a while, and examining the bridge and the fountain, we climbed the steps at the rear of the garden and sat down on a wooden bench overlooking the garden.

'What do you think?' I asked.

'It's nice,' she said. 'Are you sure no one can see us?'

'Yes, we're safe as long as we don't make any noise.'

We sat in silence for a while. 'I'm sorry about last time,' I said at length.

'What?'

'About the end of the world.'

'Oh, that's all right.'

'I sometimes get a bit…'

'Yes,' Madeleine said. 'You should calm down. It's not going to happen, anyway.'

'What makes you so sure?'

Madeleine didn't reply.

'Don't you ever have the same thoughts?' I went on.

'No,' she said, smoothing her dress.

'I envy you,' I said, wanting to kiss her. 'I'm amazed. Really.'

'Why would anyone want to destroy the world, including themselves?' asked Madeleine. 'It doesn't make sense.'

'That's what my parents always say,' I said.

'Anyway, God would never allow it to happen.'

I was quite shocked. 'God?' I said.

'Yes,' Madeleine said, annoyance in her voice. 'God.'

'I'm sorry,' I said, 'I didn't realise…'

'That I believe in God?'

'Yes.'

'There's nothing unusual about that, is there?'

'No,' I said quickly. 'Not at all… it's just… I suppose

there wasn't much… talk about God when I was growing up.'

This was true.

'Me neither,' said Madeleine. 'I had to work it out for myself. But when you think about it, it's obvious.'

'Is it? I suppose I've never really thought about it. You might be right.'

'Don't take on trust what I tell you,' Madeleine said. 'Think for yourself.'

I found this, again, slightly depressing. I decided I would become combative, since it had seemed to work earlier, in the woods.

'What about suffering?' I asked. 'Why does he allow it to happen?'

'I don't know. He has His reasons.'

'God doesn't have to explain himself?' I asked.

'That's absolutely right, Nicholas. God doesn't have to explain Himself.'

'What about…' I searched my mind for a paradox I had once heard. 'What about God being all-powerful? Doesn't that strike you as odd? For example, could God create a weight so heavy that he couldn't lift it?'

'I'm sure he could, if he wanted to.'

'But then – ' I began.

'If he wanted to, he could do it,' interrupted Madeleine. 'Anyway, Nicholas, God isn't a body-builder.'

'No,' I said.

'Don't use other people's arguments. Use your own.'

I felt the weight of Madeleine's twenty-one years to my nineteen. I was beginning to feel more and more in love with her, as if I were falling down a mine-shaft.

'Well, if God exists,' I stumbled out, 'then – will he help us?'

'Of course.'

'I mean – will he guide the human race past this crisis?'

'What crisis?' Madeleine asked blandly.

This was at the height of the cold war, you must remember, with each side only minutes away from blowing each other to atoms.

'*The* crisis,' I said, getting up. 'The arms race. Nuclear weapons. The cold war.'

'Oh, that's just nonsense,' Madeleine said. 'That will all blow over.'

I felt utterly amazed. 'Blow over?' I repeated.

Madeleine smiled at me. 'Yes, blow over,' she said.

I began pacing up and down in front of her.

'I'm sorry,' I said, 'but I don't agree. If you think we're all safe you're wrong. There are thousands of missiles pointed at us. Each one could go off at any moment. The people in control of these things are not gods, they're human beings. Perhaps one day a madman will get hold of one. It's only a matter of time.'

I gestured out towards the quarry bathed in moonlight. 'All this will go!' I declaimed loudly. 'There'll be nothing left but cockroaches!'

Suddenly a man's voice rang out. 'Hey! This is a private garden!'

I froze, one arm in the air.

'Get down here!' the voice shouted again.

Madeleine got up, a little panicked. We looked at one another, unable to speak. The voice rang out again:

'Get down here now!'

The only way out of the garden was down the steps. What to do? Remain silent? But if we did – what then? Whoever it was would come up and find us! There was no escape – we would have to go down. And so, after only a little wordless hesitation, we began slowly to descend, like guilty children. When we finally came out at the bottom, by the fountain, a man was standing there. He was a large man, about six feet tall, wearing a cap. He looked angry.

'What are you doing here?' he asked.

'Nothing,' I said.

'Are you guests?'

'No,' I said.

'Then get out!' he shouted. 'Go on! I'm sick of you people!' He grabbed at Madeleine's arm. Madeleine jerked it away. The man took a step closer, an orange scowl on his face. He reached for her again.

With lightning swiftness, Madeleine kicked the man very hard in the groin.

The man uttered a loud, agonized bark and took six skittering steps backwards. He sank to his knees on the wet flagstones, clutching himself, his head bowed in an attitude of prayer. He gave a deep, long groan.

'Come on!' shouted Madeleine.

We ran to the gap in the railing and were gone into the night.

•

It was a very strange evening. Madeleine was suddenly very animated. She seemed to have come completely alive. It was quite a remarkable transformation. Though I must just say, girls, that to kick any man in the groin is very painful and should never really be done.

As we ran, Madeleine began chattering rapidly about the man and the way he had collapsed. I was forced to admit that it had been striking. 'Did you see the look on his face!' she kept saying. 'And that noise he made!'

Half running, half walking, we came out into the main road, near the university. Soon we came into Mire Street and joined the throngs of students. Only then did I begin to think we might be safe. There were no police cars around – and even if there had been, they could not possibly have picked us out. Neither of us looked particularly distinctive or unusual. Madeleine had her heavy boots on, of course, but so did the majority of the girls.

Thoughts were tumbling through my mind. The act that Madeleine had just committed – let's be clear, girls – was an assault, and a grievous one. For all we knew, that man was still lying there on the flagstones, moaning pitifully. Though, to put the other side of the case, he had touched her first. Could this touch itself be considered an assault? It was possible. And what was going through Madeleine's mind? Was she simply thinking that he deserved everything he'd got, and that was the end of it? Did she feel nothing but delight? Not so long ago she had tried to attack me in exactly the same fashion! Did that mean that she thought that I, by rights, should be there beside him, groaning on the flagstones? In fact, what did she really think of me? Had she forgiven me? Did she even like me? Was she waiting for an opportunity to kick me again? Would her rage descend, spontaneously, out of a clear blue sky, just as it had five minutes ago? Was I destined to wind up on the end of her heavy boot?

Madeleine's Spanish eyes flashed; she laughed; her dark hair streamed behind her.

Soon we arrived at the university and began walking down the path where I had encountered Larkin. We stopped outside the Junior Common Room, where there seemed to be a disco in progress. Madeleine suggested we go in and have something to drink. I agreed. We climbed up the crowded steps to the disco on the upper floor.

In the upper room the dance floor was packed full. Everyone was in a happy mood. The music was loud and the air was full of cigarette smoke, sweat and shouted conversation. Madeleine still had a smile on her lips. We were forced closely together in the crush as we approached the bar, and I could smell her body, which was like night-flowering jasmine. As the music approached its chorus, the whole room joined in singing. The joy was so intense that there were screams from the crowd, and at that moment Madeleine and I were pressed tightly together against a pillar.

•

The kiss went on a long time. It was long, and liquid, and soft, and Madeleine seemed very gentle. I looked into her eyes, and stroked her hair. Touching her was the most delicious feeling in the world, like playing with a leopardess – one which, though you have trained it from birth, may at any moment revert to the dictates of its ancestors and sink its fangs into your flesh.

PART TWO

IT'S MY birthday. I'm forty-eight.

Perhaps I should describe this prison cell. It's about twelve feet long by eight feet wide, and it contains two bunks, an upper and a lower. Beside them, on the floor, is a mattress. That is the sum of all the furniture of the cell. The cell, then, having been originally designed to accommodate two, is now able to accommodate three. There is no toilet; if you need to use the toilet you must call down the corridor to the guards in their little room. The guards seem very courteous, and come promptly. The door of each cell has a small window. All you can see out of the window of this particular cell is the wall of the corridor opposite, where there happens to be a noticeboard with a couple of notices on it. There are around ten cells in this corridor, I think; five on each side. As far as I can tell, this corridor is for male prisoners only.

The occupants of the cell at the moment are myself, 'Beaver' and a young man I have never seen before, and whose name I don't know. This young man was naked to the waist when he was brought in. He has a tattoo of Elvis Presley on his back. This tattoo doesn't look like the work of a professional tattooist, but instead like a child's drawing: it is quite extraordinarily amateurish. It consists of a single line describing the profile of Elvis Presley's face, and extends from the base of the young man's neck to his waist. It therefore covers the whole of his back. The likeness is not good, and wouldn't be recognizable, in fact, as the face of

Elvis, had the anonymous author not signed the sketch with the word 'Elvis'.

The reason for the young man's nakedness is simple: he got extremely wet in the rain. So did I, as a matter of fact. I failed to bring any wet-weather clothing, as I mentioned, and so was completely unprepared. I didn't even bring an umbrella. I was soaked to the skin. Most of the other protesters were wearing kagools, raincoats, even plastic trousers and plastic spats to keep their feet dry. Meanwhile I was standing there, the rain sheeting into me, wearing my cotton suit. It wasn't even a wool suit. So I was utterly drenched, and on arrival at the station I had to remove my clothing so that it could be dried for me. This was all highly embarrassing, but I am glad to report that it was all achieved with a maximum of tact. I was quickly given a blanket. So I now I don't feel at all bad. I am, however, in my underpants, which are themselves quite damp.

One of the first things that happened when we arrived was that we were given a very good lunch. The guard explained that it was Sunday, and on Sundays a special effort was always made to feed the prisoners as they might expect to be fed at home. The lunch therefore consisted of two slices of roast beef, mashed potato, roast potato, Brussels sprouts, mashed swede, carrots and gravy. It tasted exactly like the meals I usually get at home. After that we were given tea.

Prison, actually, is not so bad. The most irksome thing is not the loss of clothing, or freedom, but the loss of female company. All the women have obviously been taken somewhere else, to a separate block, which must be very crowded, since the arrests were predominantly of young women.

Although: if there were women here, in this block, or even in this cell, it would be embarrassing to be dressed only in my underwear.

Now I come to think about it, of the total population of this cell, two-thirds are in our underpants: that is, myself and the young man with the Elvis tattoo. 'Beaver' is still wearing his camouflage trousers. He had wet-weather clothing, which he left at the booking-desk – as did most of the other protesters. I and the young man with the Elvis tattoo are therefore untypical.

•

One of the guards asked about me just now, and I told him about the Institute. 'From one institution to another!' he said with a laugh. I asked him what it was like spending all his time with people who have broken the law. He seemed to find the question a little strange. Then he replied as follows: 'You're just people.' This seemed to me to be a very humane remark.

(I have noticed that this particular guard can become quite sharp when it is needed. 'I've told you once,' I heard him say just now, though I couldn't see who he was speaking to.)

When we first arrived I was very tired, and so after lunch I went straight to the mattress on the floor and fell asleep. I had a very strange experience. As I was drifting off I was sure I could hear piano music. It sounded like a real piano being played somewhere in the police station – perhaps in one of the neighbouring cells. I fought to stay awake so that I could work out what was going on. Was it possible that some sort of Sunday concert had been arranged for the prisoners? It didn't sound like recorded music. I am sure I heard a couple of mistakes in the fingering. The music was very haunting, slow and soft. Finally sleep engulfed me.

•

What made me suspicious as I drifted off, I remember, was that I felt I had heard the same music before, on some forgotten occasion long ago: perhaps in childhood, or in a film, or on the radio, while lying wrapped in Madeleine's arms.

As above.

I WILL describe the protest in just a minute – though there isn't a great deal to tell – but first I ought to try to clear up a few more details.

In the early June of 1982 I finally left the shared house in Christiania Street. I bought a flat on Winterbank, a little nearer the centre of town. Both my parents – your grand-dad and nana, girls – had died earlier in the year – I will get onto that in a minute – and after the sale of the family home, all the money came to me. In those days a flat in Hull was quite reasonably priced, and so I had quite a lot of money left over. I was now quite wealthy, in fact. There were no siblings to share it with. You have no uncles and aunties, girls, I'm sorry to say.

There was nothing to keep me in Christiania Street in any case, since Madeleine was preparing to move out. She would be graduating later that month, and had already applied to the Hull social services for a job. As it happened she moved into rooms in Polder Row, not far from Christiania Street. Henry, Lara (who I still haven't told you anything about) and the young man whose name I can't remember were forced to look around for new tenants. I don't remember whether they found any, though I suppose they must have.

This was before the founding of the Institute, which occurred a couple of years later.

The flat where I was now living, on Winterbank, had an entryphone, and when the buzzer was pressed, a harsh electronic beep sounded. It commonly heralded the arrival of Madeleine. Very few other people visited me.

After she died –

I don't mean that she died, of course. That was a slip of the pen.

•

You must remember that I am writing this very quickly. There is no time to edit; no time to go back and revise; hardly even any time to think. There is only the flow, on and on, at breakneck speed, and hang the mistakes!

Of course this method of composition has its drawbacks. There are the inevitable *longeurs* which you will find a bit boring, girls, and perhaps will wish to skip, in the hope of finding something more interesting later on; and then there are the various other faults attendant on haste: the repetitions, infelicities of style, digressions, inadequacies of construction and pacing, *non sequiturs* and so on.

On the credit side of the ledger, however, this way of writing may produce moments of unintended frankness and candour. These unguarded moments might, in fact, even be the freshest passages of all, though the author may not know it at the time. These are the passages which he will have to struggle the hardest not to remove later on, since they will reveal more than he might at first have intended.

About 2.30 pm by the watch of 'Beaver'.

'Beaver' is a very likeable fellow. He is a very expansive character. He is about thirty years old and comes from Canada, I think. He has what one might describe as a powerful figure. One blow from that great arm could knock anyone out. Perhaps that is why he is so popular with the ladies. He has a warm, friendly face and a great, solid, fleshy nose. He is unshaven – though his beard is trimmed – and his hair, as I have said, is full of strange tangles. It reaches down to his shoulders. He looks quite wild. But he is obviously very intelligent. He managed to sustain a long conversation with the guard just now about something called shinty – which seems to be a traditional game of Scotland – despite being from a country, Canada, where no one plays shinty.

'Beaver' is one of those persons who can put anyone at their ease in a matter of seconds. The young man with the Elvis tattoo took to him immediately. So did the girls on the bus. I think I saw 'Beaver' with his arms around *two* of them on the back seat, one on either side. But not in any threatening or suggestive way. No, simply as a friend and travelling companion. It is quite possible, given the sort of person he is, that he hadn't even met them until that moment, on the coach, and yet there he was, with his arm round a pair of them! Such people do exist, I assure you. And why? Because his every movement made it clear that his motives were entirely chivalrous, that he had no intention of taking advantage... he was a man, and a red-blooded one, of course, but one who had long ago tamed and disciplined that side of himself... 'Beaver' is quite capable of making a flirtatious comment, but in the funniest way, with no particle of offence in it at all, so that the young ladies with him would be rocking with laughter, though at what, I don't know. I wasn't near enough to hear. When they arrested him he was doing Tai Chi exercises on the grass verge.

You must realise, girls, that what we were engaged in was very unusual. Unusual from the point of view of most ordinary people, I mean. Sitting down in the road to block traffic to a nuclear submarine base, in the year 2010… most people would think such a thing quite ridiculous. A waste of time. Most people in this country, indeed, are unsure whether Britain even *has* any nuclear weapons. They seem to think that they were abolished after the end of the Cold War.

Anyway, 'Beaver' was slowly moving into various positions, standing on one leg, and so on, when the police asked him to stop. The morning traffic coming into the base had now ground to a standstill, and the police were beginning to become impatient. When 'Beaver' refused to stop, two policemen took hold of him and led him off. As they did so 'Beaver' continued to move, very gently, an arm here, an arm there, very gracefully, like an insect that has become caught in tar.

Soon, arrests were being made *en masse*. Each campaigner was being picked up bodily and carried to a queue a little further off, where they had to wait before boarding a long line of police vehicles. This all took quite a long time. There were, I would estimate, around a hundred and fifty people sitting in the road. When it came to my turn, two policemen lifted me, one by the arms and one by the legs, so I was slung between them like a child getting the bumps. They had only carried me a few yards when one of them said to me: 'Now your mates can't see, can we put you down?'

I felt that this was an unnecessary remark; but I agreed, since I was now near the back of the queue, and didn't wish to continue lying down while everyone else was standing up.

Nearby, a policeman was holding a huge pink and white beach ball, which had materialized from God knows where.

·

That was at about ten this morning, I think.

·

Now the young man with the Elvis tattoo is regaling 'Beaver' with some story or other. The young man with the Elvis tattoo, it has now become obvious, is entirely unrelated to the blockade. The reason he is here is rather a melancholy one. Having nowhere to sleep last night, he made his way into a building site, and slept on the rough workings. When morning broke, he made his way off the site, but, as he was doing so, noticed a little shed. Thinking there might be some food inside, he broke the door down. There was nothing in there except some old Tupperware containers. However, a workman spotted him breaking into the shed, and called the police. The young man with the Elvis tattoo was arrested as he tried to hitch a ride on the road nearby. Because he has several previous convictions, he may well be handed a prison sentence, even though he didn't take anything.

The young man with the Elvis tattoo has a peculiar way of talking: he rolls his 'r's in a strange way, not with the tip of the tongue on the palate, but at the back of the throat, as in the 'ch' of 'loch'. This means that he pronounces a word such as 'rabbit' in a way more closely approximating to 'chwabbit'. This trick is almost certainly some sort of attempt to control a speech problem. Very likely he couldn't pronounce his 'r's in childhood. I imagine his parents were worried about this minor speech defect and took him to see a speech therapist. The young man with the Elvis tattoo – as a child – was then forced to substitute this 'ch' sound for the normal 'r' sound. What effort it must have taken, over the years! And I have no doubt that now he cannot speak without this noise: it is fixed, unalterable, except by an expenditure of effort equal to the expenditure needed to learn it in the first place. Possibly a greater expenditure, since habits learnt in childhood may be more difficult to unlearn than those acquired in adulthood. Perhaps it would now actually be impossible for him to stop speaking in this way, especially as he seems a rather simple young man.

Of course there is a deeper meaning to the young man's strange way of speaking. His parents loved him, and didn't want him to grow up disadvantaged by this slight problem. So they took him to a speech therapist, week after week; they encouraged him, scolded him, bribed him with sweets and presents; they threatened him, even; and finally he, an innocent boy, could not help giving way, and in the end did their bidding, bent himself to their will. Now the persistence and recalcitrance of this strange jarring habit of speech, every time it sounds out, speaks of that love and care and anxiety.

Oh! What would the parents of the young man with the Elvis tattoo say if they could see him now? Sitting in a police cell, telling some dull story – how they would weep!

Around 3.15 pm.

IN A prison one is of course in an all-male environment, and one's thoughts naturally turn in all sorts of strange directions. The reality of prison life is that one is confronted by certain features of our lives that one does not always encounter very often in one's ordinary existence.

•

I realise that I didn't quite finish my thought above. It is difficult to write properly, girls, sitting on this mattress with all the noise of the prison around me; even more difficult than on the coach, where I had to cope with the jolting, and the disturbance of radios, talk and so on. For example, there was a terrible commotion a few cells down just now. A voice began screaming 'Take it out, Mike! Take it out!' Two guards rushed to the scene and there was the noise of the door being unlocked; then a scuffle and some shouts. Then all was quiet. I have no idea what it was all about, nor what the 'it' referred to, nor how 'it' could be taken out, at least out of the cell, which was surely locked when the cry went up.

However, to the point.

After Madeleine left me I began to have the first of my hallucinations. They were of quite an ordinary variety, girls, and I am glad to say that things calmed down a lot later. The first hallucinations concerned the entryphone. I would often be awakened by the characteristic loud electronic buzz of this entryphone, and would spring out of bed, go to the wall and pick up the handset. 'Hello? Hello?' I would cry. But there was never any reply; only a faint electronic susurration, and perhaps the noise of a passing car. Realising that I had been the victim of a hallucination, I would go back to bed. Occasionally, however, the sound was so real-seeming that instead of going back to bed I would go to the bay window and look out, to see if anyone was there. This would generally be in the middle of the night: the street would be deserted, and moonlight could be seen silvering the roofs of the houses opposite. Sometimes going to the window was not enough. Sometimes I imagined, in my half-woozy state, that someone might be hiding outside, close to the door, under the portico, where they couldn't be seen from my first floor window; and so I would quickly put on my trousers, tiptoe down the stairs and open the front door. Needless to say, no one was ever there. After standing for a while in the moonlight, I would trudge back upstairs and drop back into bed.

Unfortunately these auditory hallucinations were not confined to the entryphone buzzer: I would also imagine that the phone was ringing. Immediately on waking it would go through my mind that it might be Madeleine, calling me for who knows what reason. I would tear myself from the bed, jump up and dash to the phone. But when I picked it up there was never anything but the hum of the dial tone. Sometimes I would stand there for a while, listening to the tone, still half-asleep, unable to believe that I had really not heard the phone ringing, so real had it sounded. I would put the phone down and sit at my desk waiting for whoever it was to call again. But there was never any further call; and so eventually I would creep back to bed.

In the first few years without Madeleine, both my waking and my sleeping life were utterly full of her.

This was quite terrible: to have her with me constantly, to want her constantly, and yet to have no prospect of seeing her, hearing her voice, or holding her: and yet I wonder if I did not, in some deep region of my heart, choose this torture, since to forget her, and surrender myself to the blankness of life without her, would have been even worse than the torment of remembering her.

THIS GAOL seems to have a soporific effect. I dozed off just now for a moment. Of course, I got very little sleep last night. It is difficult to sleep on a coach. In any case, I nodded off on the mattress. I had a very amusing dream. It was of Professor Wo, of Sai Kun University. I dreamt that Professor Wo was there in the cell with us. He looked very anxious, but in the dream I realised that this was not attributable to his imprisonment, but to the fact that he was worried about his upcoming speech. I reassured him, saying that we were all looking forward to hearing him speak, that I was sure it would be a great success, that he was greatly admired in Hull, and that there was absolutely nothing to worry about. The facilities at the Institute, I told him, were of world-class standard. He need have no concerns that the Institute might be in a state of partial completion when he arrived, or, God forbid, that it might not exist at all. If that were the case he would certainly have read all about it in the *Renmin Ribao*. At that moment I saw an expression of deep astonishment cross his features. It had evidently not occurred to him that the Institute might not exist. He had merely been worrying about his lecture. Now I had added a further layer of worry, that he might arrive and there would be nowhere to give his lecture – nowhere to go, nowhere to stay, no one to talk to, and nothing to do. At this point I remember making things very much worse by asking him, I'm afraid, a very inappropriate question, in his native language: 'Have you had many lovers?' (I am able to dream in Chinese, which is often taken as a sign of some fluency in the language. For example I had a dream recently in which I was asked to tell the time in Chinese on a gigantic clock.) It seemed that Professor Wo was on the point of replying to this inappropriate question, inappropriate or not, when Hannah walked past and exclaimed breezily '*I* have!' She was fully dressed. And at that moment I woke up, though I was surprised to find Professor Wo still there in the cell with me. 'So you're here,' I said to him. 'I'm very glad. You must have been on the coach. I have some notes here to prove that the Institute is a real place.' I handed him a big sheaf of drawings, several of which spilled from my hands onto the floor. 'These are the architectural plans for the Institute,' I said. 'This big blueprint shows the entire Institute in detail.' I unfolded it, but it seemed to open out to a size bigger than the entire cell. Finally I had unfolded all of the blueprint, but it was buckled and impossible to get a good look at. Then I did at last swim back into waking consciousness. 'Beaver' was sleeping on the top bunk and the young man with the Elvis tattoo was awake and listening to a radio.

.

I suppose it is because I have been writing about Hannah that I had the dream above: I generally do not dream about her.

Since Hannah has been mentioned I would like to put on record that I think Hannah may have been in love with me, and not just because she appeared before me in her underwear. In fact Hannah was always doing the most provocative things, though I was always uncertain as to whether they were intended to be provocative or not. For example, in a casual discussion about a friend's wedding, Hannah once admitted to me privately that she could not accept an invitation to be a bridesmaid, because bridesmaids were supposed to be virgins, and she was not a virgin. She was rather out of breath at the time, because we had been dancing together in a large hall; in fact we had been the only couple dancing.

Or was that a dream? I feel sure that it did happen, but certain elements of it are dreamlike — for example the large hall and our aloneness; and anyone can see that it is rather unusual to be dancing alone in a huge hall. I certainly cannot recall any other occasion when I have done it. Anyhow, Hannah, as I have said, breathlessly admitted that she was not a virgin, then regarded me with a somewhat stern eye. As in our other encounters, that stern gaze seemed to suggest something quite other than you might expect. If anyone else told you breathlessly that they were not a virgin, after having danced alone with you, you might be forgiven for thinking that the essence of the communication was… something to do with that aspect, at least, of human affairs. However, in Hannah's case, her words seemed to be an allegory for something else entirely. She seemed to be saying something such as: 'I gladly throw off all mental and spiritual bonds, and cast aside all love for the world of men, Nicholas, because you and I will one day kneel in the presence of the Logos.'

As above.

BUT I do keep going on about 'Beaver' and the young man with the Elvis tattoo, and all the others, as if they were the real subjects of this diary, which they are not. Madeleine is the real subject of this diary. I also seem to have spent a great deal of time explaining how matters stood *vis à vis* Hannah and Alice and the girl who always said 'Aren't you going to *do* something?' I really should make more of an effort to show you how important Madeleine was to me.

Perhaps I might share a memory of her, therefore.

In the late spring of 1982, Madeleine asked me to meet her at the airport. She had just returned from Italy, where she'd been attending a wedding. I don't drive, so I had arranged for a car with a driver, at some expense, for the fifty-mile round trip.

As we drove from Humberside airport back to Hull, Madeleine seemed very tired and disinclined to talk. I had at first rather foolishly got into the front seat with the driver, feeling obscurely that the driver shouldn't be left alone in the front of the car, but I soon realised that this was rather absurd, and asked the driver to stop the car while I changed seats and got in the back next to Madeleine. The driver was an older man of about sixty years of age, of Asian extraction, very pleasant, who readily agreed: thus I got into the back seat and sat close to Madeleine, who immediately put her head on my shoulder and fell asleep. I put my arm around her. Her hair tickled my neck and her body rose and fell against mine, and I was enfolded in the fragrance of her body. It felt almost as if she had brought the voluptuous warmth of the Mediterranean back to England with her. The car purred: all was peace. I wasn't sleepy and in any case wanted to stay awake for as long as possible, feeling the warmth and scent of her body and her trustful repose against me. She slept on and on, all the way back to Hull. I think I will never forget the peace of that drive, how warm and how close we were, and how I felt that Madeleine and I had finally arrived at a perfect understanding which nothing could ever dislodge. Just as we came into Hull, the driver stopped to get some petrol. Madeleine woke up, stretched herself, and asked me to get some milk, since she didn't have any at home. I went to the station shop to buy some, and came back holding milk, a small box of tea, and some biscuits. When I returned to the car, the driver saw what I was carrying and delivered himself of a harmless remark. He said quietly, half to himself: 'All the materials for a midnight feast.' When I heard these words it struck me forcefully that this driver, many times in the past, had enjoyed midnight feasts with his loved ones. He wasn't merely a driver, but a husband, father, lover. He was very familiar with the innocence of a midnight feast. I looked at Madeleine and saw that she too had heard this remark, but that she hadn't seen its significance. I almost felt like asking the driver to join us in our midnight feast when we got back, since I felt a sudden kinship with him; but of course to do such a thing would have been utterly ridiculous. The essence of the feast was that Madeleine and I should be alone, together. I hadn't seen Madeleine for nearly two weeks, and had barely exchanged a word with her since she had arrived. How, then, could I ask a driver to share our first moments together in all that time? It would almost be a betrayal. But still, it seemed a dirty world, in which it was impossible to invite a driver in for tea and biscuits.

Then a further revelation was granted me: perhaps the chief revelation of the entire incident. I suddenly realised that our roles were not quite as fixed as I had thought. In a reality very close to the one we currently inhabited, I was the driver, and the driver was in the back with Madeleine. This strange idea came, as it were, out of nowhere, utterly changing my mood. The future suddenly seemed very uncertain. Today, granted, I had Madeleine in my arms, and was shortly to share a midnight feast with her. But in an eyeblink I might have none of the materials for that feast, including, and especially, of course, Madeleine herself. The only feast I would have would be a feast of memories and longings. She would be with someone else, not the driver, of course, but someone other than me. Her warmth and hair and scent, which only a few minutes ago had seemed so real and so permanent, would be swept away by a sudden whirlwind and would never come back. I felt the tang of that future aloneness. I sensed that however lonely I became, I could expect no pity, and that no one would ever invite me in for tea and biscuits.

•

Actually that is rather too much. I don't think it was really quite that much of a revelation: I have made too much of it. But the mood of the whole evening did later change markedly. I don't think I can tell this to the girls. When Madeleine and I arrived at Christiania Street and got out of the car, and we were retrieving our luggage from the boot, the driver touched Madeleine. At least, I found out later that he did: at the time I didn't notice anything. It was only afterwards, after I had paid him and he had driven off, that Madeleine mentioned it. In fact I had to draw it out of her. She was so stiff, I knew something must be wrong. He had touched her, so she said, on her behind, though not with his hand but with his body. I asked if she was sure he hadn't simply brushed up against her as he was helping to retrieve the luggage, and she said that she was sure: it was deliberate.

'Why would he do that?' I asked.

'Don't be stupid, Nicholas,' Madeleine said.

'You mean he wanted...?'

'Yes!'

'Are you sure it wasn't an accident?'

'Yes,' she said, setting her lips. 'I should report him.'

Madeleine was standing up at her little kitchen worktop, in her room with the red and orange cushions, glowering, her luggage unpacked. Our reunion was forgotten. Suddenly she went out into the corridor to the pay phone.

'What are you going to do?' I asked.

'Give me the name of that car company,' she said.

'No, don't!' I said.

Madeleine frowned savagely at me. 'He didn't touch you, did he?'

I gave her the name. Madeleine called the operator and got the number. Then she dialled the car company. But there was no reply: it was late at night, and the company was not a cab service, as such, but a private operator. Madeleine then started dialling another number, evidently a minicab company. She spoke to the operator and mentioned the name of the car company.

I was astonished. 'Surely you're not going to go out again at this time of night?' I said.

'That's my business, Nicholas,' Madeleine snapped.

She went into the bathroom. I followed and stood in the kitchen, which still had, above the cooker, a painting of an ichthyosaur. My stomach was throbbing. After a minute I went to the bathroom door.

'Please!' I said through the door. 'This is our first night back! Can't you forget it?'

'No!' Madeleine shouted.

The doorbell rang. It was the minicab. Madeleine marched out of the bathroom, her bag on her shoulder, still dressed in her travel clothes. She ran down the hall to the front door. 'Wait here!' she shouted.

I ran after her and out of the house, reaching the minicab just as the door was closing. Madeleine nearly shut the door on my arm. I got in beside her.

Now, again, we were both together on the back seat, but this time the mood was very different. Madeleine sat bolt upright, her face grim. I didn't try to touch her, naturally. We drove for about ten minutes and stopped in front of the car company offices. It was not actually a business at all, but a private house, rather shabby, on a one-way street. The windows were unlit. The car that had brought us from the airport was outside: a long green car. The airport driver had obviously returned, and had retired to bed. I couldn't help marvelling at Madeleine's efficiency. I felt sure that if it had been me I would never have tracked the airport driver down with such speed.

Madeleine now asked the minicab driver to wait, and we got out. She strode to the front door of the house and banged on it. After perhaps half a minute, lights came on in the hall, and the door opened. It was the airport driver, the Asian man. He looked very surprised.

Madeleine reached out and touched his sleeve.

'Do you like that?' she asked.

The driver didn't seem displeased, though he didn't speak. Suddenly I was convinced that Madeleine was right, and that the touch he had given her had been deliberate. I felt a fool, though for a rather strange reason: I had considered sharing tea and biscuits with this man. I now saw how utterly wrong I was to have considered it, and how little hope there was for me. I would probably persist for my whole life in feeling sorry for men who said, dreamily, 'All the materials for a midnight feast.'

It is perhaps unnecessary to describe what Madeleine did next, except that as soon as she had done it, the minicab driver got out of his seat and ran over to us. 'Hey!' he shouted at Madeleine. Madeleine was still looking down at the Asian man. The Asian man had slid down the door-frame and was making a choking sound. The minicab driver grabbed Madeleine by the shoulder and span her around. Madeleine then did the same thing to the minicab driver, though this time she used her knee. It was the first time I had seen the use of the knee. The minicab driver, without uttering a sound, collapsed instantly. He seemed lost in thought.

Suddenly we heard footsteps from inside the house. A woman in a nightdress appeared in the door, holding a hand to her mouth. 'I'll call the police!' she shrieked.

Madeleine calmly pointed down at the Asian man. 'This man sexually harassed me,' she stated flatly. She turned. 'And so did this man.' She pointed at the minicab driver, who had managed to stumble part of the way back to his car; I, however, was close by, and seemed as though she were pointing at me.

The evening some time: I really don't know.

I MUST say I am an ardent supporter of feminism. It does rather leave open the question, though: what exactly is the role of males?

To put the question another way: if any conceivable job can be done by women, and if women are in future able to bear children without the intervention of males – which I think you will admit may well happen – and if – and here is my central point – the evil done by men outweighs the good, why retain men at all?

The obvious answer is that women will wish to keep men for a certain biological function that is related to, but not necessarily resultant in, reproduction.

But will they, in fact? Will it really be worth the bother? It seems that many women are quite disdainful of men's efforts in this area, and regard it as beneath their dignity to submit to... They might instead prefer... Or perhaps I might put it another way: they might instead prefer...

5.45 pm by the watch of 'Beaver'.

'BEAVER' ENGAGED me in conversation just now. He had seen me scribbling and asked if I was writing a letter. I told him I was writing a diary. He asked me if it was about the protest. I said it was. He then rather surprised me by asking if I would read some of it aloud to him. I said that I would when I had finished; he replied that that was 'cool'. But this journal I am writing for you, girls, isn't really about the protest, as such – or only in parts – and the parts that are about the protest contain comments that can't easily be shared. For example, I have talked quite a lot about the young women on the coach, and, actually, rather a lot about 'Beaver' himself, and his trousers. I certainly couldn't read that to him. Though I did, as I recall, write that he was a likeable young man. Is it possible he has read some of this diary while I've been asleep? Is that why he asked me to read from it, knowing as he does that the only sections that directly concern the protest mention him? Is that what is at the root of it?

What would he say if I did in fact, in a spirit of camaraderie, read him the section regarding the trousers? Would he find it funny? Would he in fact find it all highly amusing – he is, as I have said, a very genial sort – and laugh, and then actually *tell* me why he is wearing the camouflage trousers? Could this in fact be my opportunity to find out? I wrote a while ago that it was impossible to imagine asking him why he was wearing the trousers; I had resigned myself, in fact, to never knowing; and yet in a few short hours, everything has changed! Now I have a golden opportunity to find out!

But then again, perhaps he wouldn't take it so well. Perhaps he would be offended, and not say a word. God forbid, he might become angry, perhaps even violent. 'Beaver' is a tall, well-built man. I couldn't rely on the young man with the Elvis tattoo for support. He and 'Beaver' have struck up something of a friendship. I am now forced to think about the possibility I mentioned previously – that he has already read the diary, and the sections referring to himself. Could his request that I read it aloud be so that he could then, legitimately, express his anger? He could hardly admit to having surreptitiously read my notebook. He might wish to trick me, therefore, into reading the relevant passages out loud, so that he could then express his indignation. His intent, seemingly benign, is in fact malevolent.

It seems therefore that I will never know about the camouflage trousers.

•

To my astonishment the following conversation has just taken place between 'Beaver' and the young man with the Elvis tattoo.

'What's with the trousers?' the young man with the Elvis tattoo said (although he actually said something more like 'tchwousers').

'Beaver' laughed. 'Army surplus,' he said.

'You in the army?' the young man with the Elvis tattoo asked.

'No,' 'Beaver' replied.

'My uncle's in the army,' the young man with the Elvis tattoo said. 'He's a t—.' (The word he used wasn't very polite, girls.)

After that they began talking of other things. But how strange! It was almost as if things were turning out just so as to enlighten me about the trousers! *First* I thought that I would never know anything about them, *then* I realised I had an opportunity to find out, *then* this hope was dashed, and *then* the conversation above took place, informing me exactly why 'Beaver' was wearing them! This is exactly the sort of thing that, if you found it in a novel, you wouldn't believe a word of!

Except of course that I don't really feel any the wiser. I now feel sure that 'Beaver' has not read my diary, or if he has, that he doesn't harbour any particular grudge against me, which is a great relief; but I am not particularly satisfied with his answer to the young man with the Elvis tattoo about the camouflage trousers. It doesn't really explain anything. Naturally 'Beaver' picked the trousers up at an army surplus store – where else? The information is tautological. And it seems highly unlikely that 'Beaver' will elaborate further, at least to the young man with the Elvis tattoo. I will have to draw him out myself if I want to know more. And I don't really see how I can do it. Even if I read him the section in my diary to do with my perplexity about his trousers – not that I would go that far, now, I think – his response will quite possibly remain simply what it was to the young man with the Elvis tattoo: that he picked them up at an army surplus store. That is, after all, sufficient in itself, on a certain level. It needs no elaboration.

About 6 pm.

I WOULD just like to mention a rather funny thing that occurred shortly after the incident I have described with the two drivers. It was when Madeleine and I went together to see a play at the student theatre.

It was one of those plays where everyone sits on the floor, rather than in seats: a 'modern' play, so called. Madeleine and I were at the very front. The play consisted of the remarks of two actors sitting in dustbins. Every so often one of the lids of the dustbins would open and an actor would pop up and speak. The lid would then bang shut and the other actor would pop up.

It was all quite interesting, but I soon began to feel rather uncomfortable. I hadn't had any lunch or dinner, and my stomach was rumbling. The play contained frequent long silences, and at these moments the rumbling was painfully audible. It wasn't just me who could hear it: it was quite audible, I was sure, to the people either side of me – who included Madeleine, of course – and to the actors, and to the entire front section of the audience, in fact. I began to worry that the actors would comment on it. It was that sort of a play, where anything goes. But after enduring it for ten minutes I realised what the trouble was. It wasn't merely the fact that I was hungry. Saliva was forming copiously in my mouth, and each time a mass of saliva collected I would swallow it. Each time I swallowed it my stomach would begin digesting it with terrible roars. If I could prevent myself from swallowing, then, my stomach would stop rumbling. But I dreadfully wanted to swallow: and when your mouth is full of saliva, and the back of your throat is parched and dry, it is all you can do to resist. So I sat there, quite oblivious to the play, trying desperately not to swallow, my mouth rapidly filling – to the point of running over, almost – with a great mass of saliva. I knew that if I swallowed this mass – there must have been almost a cupful in there – the response from my stomach would be unprecedented. It would pounce on the saliva and let out a roar of terrifying proportions, one that would be heard throughout the theatre, possibly even reaching the foyer.

I was presented therefore with a choice of evils. Either swallow the saliva and suffer the consequences, or leave the theatre. I was just about to decide on this latter alternative, and stand up – perhaps with a whisper to Madeleine – and walk out, very probably dribbling saliva as I went – making a complete fool of myself – when I realised how I could save the situation. Why not, in fact, just void the saliva out of my mouth onto the floor? Yes... it was dark, and no one would see. And I think I was about to do this when an obvious objection presented itself. At the end of the play, when the lights came up, everyone would be able to see this patch of spit, and they would wonder why it was there. And they wouldn't have far to look.

I was now in despair. Of course I couldn't just sit there all night spitting onto the floor. What had I been thinking? I would have to revert to my original plan: walk out of the theatre while the play was in progress, risking the gibes of the actors. And I was just about to do this when the true solution came to me. Instead of voiding the saliva onto the floor, I would void it into the inside of my jacket. No one would see. If I did it carefully, it wouldn't show on the outside – the spit would only stain the lining.

So, cautiously, as inconspicuously as possible, opening the flap of my jacket a little, and putting my head down, I discharged the contents of my mouth into the lining, letting the spit run down the entire length of the inside of the jacket to give it a good chance of soaking in before it reached the tops of my trousers. There was an awful lot of it. Some of it did indeed run all the way down to the tops of my trousers, but I didn't think it mattered because I knew that when I stood up the bottom of the jacket would conceal the stain. I did this five or six times. Each time my mouth filled up, I let the saliva pour down into the inside of my jacket. I seemed to have an inexhaustible supply of it. And it worked! My stomach ceased rumbling! I had defeated, not only my stomach, but also my profligate salivary glands, which, after filling up my mouth five or six times, gave up the ghost and ceased production entirely. I was left with an achingly dry mouth, but that could be endured. I no longer faced the prospect of being embarrassed in front of hundreds of people.

There was only one thing: I knew that the actors could see me dribbling into my coat. However, I doubted whether they would remark on it. I don't know why. I felt quite relaxed over this aspect of the situation.

When the play ended, and the lights came up, I was satisfied to see that although the inside of my jacket was soaking, the outside was barely affected.

•

Reading what I have written above, there doesn't seem much point to it. There is nothing about Madeleine in it at all. It's all about me. I may flag it for deletion.

•

Were any of the other members of that hundred-strong audience spitting into their jackets? Somehow I doubt it. And yet, if not, why not? Am I so different…? Everyone has a digestive system… everyone has salivary glands… many members of the audience that night wouldn't have eaten dinner… and yet I was the only one doing this ludicrous thing, slowly spitting into my jacket, like a lizard… and proud of it! How stupid! This was why the actors could not comment. It was too abnormal, too reptilian, to be comprehensible… even by two people sitting in dustbins. What did I keep in there, that had to be fed with spit? It was too bizarre to risk a comment. I was beyond the pale even of mockery.

·

Actually, I remember, one strange thing did happen at that play. At the end, no one applauded. We simply got up and filed out. The play had lasted over two hours, during which time the actors had spoken hundreds, perhaps thousands of lines. But the play had so thoroughly undermined the conventions of the theatre that somehow it seemed inappropriate to applaud. So instead we simply filed out, perhaps a little demoralized, perhaps a little embarrassed, perhaps rather wondering whether we had done the right thing, and leaving the actors sitting in their dustbins in the dark.

6.30 pm or thereabouts.

MY PROBLEMS with Madeleine began for a rather surprising reason: Dr Closer. This would have been just before Madeleine left the university.

The first time I realised that something serious was happening was on the day of the local elections. Madeleine and I were having lunch together at the café at the university: she had about an hour before her lecture. I'd brought a kite with me, and thought it might be fun if we had some lunch and then went down to the lake to fly it. I suggested this to Madeleine, and she agreed. But just as we were about to leave we saw Dr Closer approaching our table.

Madeleine, I should mention, had struck up something of a friendship with Dr Closer. Whereas I always called Dr Closer by her formal title, that is, 'Dr Closer', Madeleine soon started calling her by her first name, that is, 'Caroline'. It wasn't unusual for students to call the lecturers by their first names, but I somehow didn't feel it proper, even though Dr Closer was in the habit of kissing me full on the lips. (In fact, I continued calling her 'Dr Closer' against the express wish of Dr Closer herself. I remember the occasion – we were sitting in her garden, and Dr Closer said to me from her deckchair: 'Nicholas, call me Caroline.' I frowned and shook my head. 'No,' I said, 'I think I should call you Dr Closer.' She didn't press me: I think she respected my decision. I think she divined too that there was a certain perversity in me, a certain tendency to do things that I knew were against my own best interests; and yet knew also that this tendency in me should not be opposed, but instead allowed to run its course. I also think, though, looking back on it, that I should have done as she said, and called her 'Caroline'. I wish that Dr Closer had, on that autumn afternoon, got up from her deckchair, walked the few steps over to me, knelt in front of me on the damp grass, brought her beautiful face close to mine, and said to me in a soft voice: 'Nicholas, I want you to call me Caroline, and I will not get up from my knees until you call me Caroline.' Such an act would have been entirely consistent with Dr Closer's character, because, as I hope I have made clear, girls, she was a woman of extraordinary sympathy and insight, as well as one liable to outbursts of rapacious vindictiveness. And I would have capitulated immediately. All my awkwardness would have evaporated like dew on a summer morning; and perhaps things wouldn't later have taken the turn they did.

However, all this is mere speculation.)

'Hello, you two,' Dr Closer said, sitting down at the table. 'What are you plotting?'

'Nothing,' Madeleine said, smiling.

'Well,' Dr Closer continued, her eyes on Madeleine, 'Are you at least going to vote today?'

'I'm going to,' Madeleine said, 'sometime this evening.'

'I can give you a lift to the polling station if you like,' Dr Closer said.

Madeleine smiled again. 'After my lecture?'

'All right,' said Dr Closer. 'About four? Meet me outside the union building.'

Madeleine nodded. And at precisely the same moment, both of them turned to look at me.

It was at this moment, girls, that I understood that Madeleine was much closer than I had realised to Dr Closer.

Of course the question of voting and lifts was mere froth.

Dr Closer did in fact ask me, immediately after she and Madeleine had simultaneously turned their gazes onto me, whether I too would like a lift. But there was a perceptible pause just before she did it. It was obvious that the offer was insincere. She wished to be alone with Madeleine, and Madeleine, it was obvious, wished to be alone with Dr Closer. Dr Closer's offer to me was for form's sake, to prevent the conversation descending into utter barbarity. I was expected to say that I didn't want a lift, or that I had already voted. I was expected to see that I was not wanted. It was rather like what had happened to the girlfriend of 'Dick'. I was expected to acquiesce, even participate in my own undoing. Dr Closer, right in front of me, was taking Madeleine away from me. We all knew what was happening. But couldn't Dr Closer see that she didn't really need Madeleine, and that I did? I am sure she could. So why was she taking Madeleine from me? And why, if that was what she intended, had she asked me to call her 'Caroline'? I was like the schoolboy, set apart from the rest of humanity by his suffering. Henceforth, I was privileged. If I could find the words, I could say anything I liked. I could tell Dr Closer that she was old and ugly. I could say that she was forty-seven and Madeleine twenty-one, and that it wouldn't last. I could tell them that they disgusted me. I could be forgiven the vilest outburst. I was expected, in fact, to say something wounding, forbidden – and I knew that this terrible thing would go completely unchallenged.

'I think voting is a waste of time,' I said.

Dr Closer examined me with thoughtful eyes. 'Yes, you're probably right,' she said.

I stood up. 'We're all going to die anyway.'

Dr Closer appeared to consider.

'I think…' she began, but I cut her off.

'I'm going for a walk by the lake,' I said. I looked at Madeleine and saw that she knew quite well what I meant – to fly the kite.

Then I left, without saying goodbye to Dr Closer.

•

There was a large open area down at the lake, girls, mainly of scrub. I unwrapped the kite and put it together quite easily. The day was perfect for kite-flying: dry, and with a light wind. I felt sure that Madeleine would soon join me.

I took a good look at the assembled kite. It was in the shape of an eagle, and was made of paper and wood strips. It looked more like a decorative object than a proper kite designed for flying, but it was definitely a kite, as there were strings attached to it.

There weren't many other people around as I held the kite up and threw it into the breeze, the spool of thread unwinding in my left hand. The kite caught the wind quickly and pulled away, but, as the string tightened, the kite seemed to sense that something was wrong, and instead of soaring skywards, heeled over and crashed smartly to the ground. I went after it and picked it up. I checked it to see that the strings on either wing were of the same length and met in the middle: they both seemed in order. I tried again. The same thing happened: a quite sharp pull and a plummet to the ground. Something was obviously wrong. I examined the kite again, this time with more care. Of course, I am not an expert on kites. I couldn't see anything the matter. I tried again. This time there was a stronger gust of wind and the kite strained hard away from me, trying to fly, but despite all the encouragement I could give it – running, pulling the strings – again it turned over and fell to the earth with a jolt.

This was all very discouraging. It wouldn't have mattered if Madeleine had been there, but she wasn't. Fifteen minutes had now passed, and she hadn't joined me. She knew exactly where I was, and yet she preferred to chat with Dr. Closer. I felt anger, stronger now, rising in me.

Time was passing and the kite wouldn't fly. Time was running out. Did Madeleine understand how I felt? I tried the kite again, this time modifying the strings so that they were asymmetrical: again it crashed, in exactly the same way. Soon Madeleine would be going into her lecture. I flew the kite again and again, catching the wind on almost every occasion: every time the kite fell with a thump.

After half an hour, I collected up the kite and began to walk home. Near the car park, on the way out of the University, I broke the kite in half. I tried stuffing it in a rubbish bin, but the bin was full, so I left half of it protruding out of the top. I cut myself painfully on one of the bamboo splinters. I wondered if Madeleine would see the kite as she left that day.

•

It's difficult to write these things, even after all this time. Funny! How something that happened twenty-eight years ago – more than a quarter of a century! – can bring back these feelings. Of course, it's not as if I was caught up in a war or something. I was in the habit of constantly reminding myself of that fact, in those days, when things got very bad: I'm still alive, I would tell myself, I still have arms and legs, and hands and feet… I can still breathe and run… I still have food and shelter.

Actually there was a sequel to the event with the kite. I didn't actually go home, as I have said. I was going to go home, but I stopped. I felt that I couldn't just go back to the flat. I turned around and began walking back to the cafeteria. I was now in a state near madness, and my finger was throbbing painfully. I knew that if I found Madeleine and Dr Closer together, still in the café, I would say or do something that not even the schoolboy could be forgiven for. I arrived at the café and pushed through the revolving door. I walked to the table where we had been sitting. It was empty.

Madeleine had not bothered to come down to the lake, and had spent the whole lunch hour with Dr Closer – or 'Caroline'. Then they had left together.

If she had gone to her lecture, then I would find her there. I ran out of the café and along the concourse towards the social sciences faculty. Madeleine's class number was posted outside the lecture theatre. I looked through a panel in the door. A lecture was in progress. A young man with ginger hair was pacing up and down in front of an overhead projector. I quietly entered the lecture hall, sat down at the rear of the hall, and began to scrutinize, in turn, each of the hundred-or-so heads, from the back.

To my surprise the lecturer stopped talking. 'Hello?' he said. The entire lecture hall now turned around to face me.

'Hello?' I replied.

'Are you a student on this course?'

I stood up. My head was whirling.

'No,' I said. 'I dropped out.'

There was a great roar of laughter. The blood beat in my cheeks.

'I'm afraid only students on this course may attend lectures,' the lecturer said.

'Is Madeleine here?' I asked.

Again there was a bewildering howl of laughter.

The lecturer now looked quite peeved. 'This is not a social event,' he said. 'Please wait outside.'

Unfortunately for him, the lecturer was unable to see that the incident in the café with Dr Closer, and then the kite-flying incident, had left me in a state of near lunacy. He had chosen to forget, if he had ever known, what love is. I felt my neck and shoulders filling with a rigid substance.

'Your lecture is a social event,' I said, without thinking. 'It's about sociology, after all.'

The laughter that greeted this artless remark was, again, very loud. I widened my eyes in ghastly fashion.

'Please leave,' the lecturer said.

'I'm going,' I said. 'I can see Madeleine isn't here.'

There was silence.

I turned and walked out.

•

As far as I know Madeleine didn't see the kite in the waste bin. She never mentioned it, anyway. And that was the end of it all, girls. Sometimes when you fall in love it doesn't work out and it hurts terribly, and it takes a long time for the wound to heal, but eventually things improve. I was lucky: soon after all this, I had the Institute. And then you came along! And I have counted my blessings every day since.

•

Was Madeleine with Dr Closer that day?

I asked Madeleine later on what she had done after lunch and she said she had not gone to her lecture after all.

167

Where, then, had she gone? She had gone to visit a friend, she said. Of course I found this answer highly suspicious. I thought of asking for the friend's name, but eventually decided not to. I had a horror of finding she had lied.

Madeleine later found out that I had gone to her lecture and that I hadn't found her there; she was given a full report of my behaviour in the lecture hall by her friends.

Just after dinner.

WE'VE JUST had dinner, rather late. The dinner itself wasn't quite as good as lunch. It was lasagna. There was no dessert.

After dinner.

Shortly afterwards Hannah Closer had an eighteenth birthday party, and I was invited. Madeleine was invited too, but I didn't see much of her at the party. I suppose I went with the idea in my mind that I might talk to Madeleine or Dr Closer and find out what was going on.

I should describe Dr Closer's house. Dr Closer – and her husband, Mr Closer – lived in a detached property in a leafy area of Hull, on the outskirts of the town. It was unadjoined by any other property, up a long curving drive, screened from the neighbourhood by stands of trees. My own upbringing was quite comfortable, girls, in that my parents were quite well off – I myself, as I have said, was by then quite well off – but Dr Closer and Mr Closer existed in an atmosphere of culture that my parents could not have imagined. The house was full of books, for example: every room, almost, was lined with bookcases. This was something my own upbringing sadly lacked. My own father had very little in the way of books, except for a few popular novels: he was a businessman, not an academic. And it wasn't only the books: in the hallway, at the foot of the stairs, was a large wooden sculpture with a frankly erotic subject. And on the wall, in the stairwell, was an original oil suggestive of a Chagall – perhaps it even *was* a Chagall.

I arrived a little late. The whole house was already full of young people – packed, almost – and it was a very large house. I imagine that there were at least two hundred people there. I recognized only a few, and so I was content simply to find a drink and wander here and there, looking around, examining the pictures on the walls, the books and furnishings, and watching the occasionally madcap behaviour of my fellow guests. There were so many of them, and they were so young, that they were beginning to do quite noticeable damage to the house. For example, there were already numerous stains on the carpet and furnishings. Cigarettes were being smoked by the hundred, and there were not sufficient ashtrays. The ash was therefore being deposited directly onto the floor, or into the palms of girls' hands – and then onto the floor. Butts of cigarettes lay everywhere. Drunken, dancing boys – this was around ten o'clock – were careering into things while the girls looked on and screamed with laughter. There was no deliberate attempt to damage the house, of course, but purely through the attrition of so many bodies, damage was nevertheless being done. At one point I saw a girl perch herself on the edge of an ornate sink in the bathroom – this I could see through the open door – and the sink, with a loud crack, came away from the wall and flopped forward, held up only by its plumbing. The girl, startled, hopped off, then looked about her and laughed.

Through all of this moved the figure of Mr Closer. Mr Closer was a small man with a mordant look. Although unremarkable in appearance, his behaviour was very remarkable. He was observing his house being destroyed and doing nothing to stop it. He was not, for example, scurrying around with a mop or ashtrays. He was not picking up the pieces of broken ornament or chiding the girl for breaking the sink, nor attempting to stop any of the guests engaged in wild dancing or amorous activity. Once or twice I saw him wince, but that was all. His restraint was quite astonishing. No one was taking any notice of him. I was the only one observing him.

Suddenly my attention was drawn to an outlandish spectacle. Two lads, both drunk, had decided that it would be amusing to steal the painting in the stairwell – the one that may or may not have been a Chagall. Perhaps they were students of art history. I doubt whether they truly wished to *steal* it, as such. In fact subsequent events showed that they had no real plan to do so. They simply lifted the painting from its hook on the wall and began carrying it, laughing, down the stairs. The painting was about five feet square and needed two pairs of hands. I looked around to see if Mr Closer or Dr Closer were anywhere in evidence; and was astonished to see that Mr Closer was calmly watching them, his back against the jamb of the front room door.

Once the boys had delivered the painting safely to the ground floor, they hesitated. To walk out of the house with the painting would be to miss the rest of the party. They consulted briefly, then propped the canvas up against the banisters and sauntered off. The painting remained there for the rest of the evening. Mr Closer had not said or done anything, and yet I had the feeling that his quietism had somehow shaped the incident.

Then a further insight was afforded me. It all became suddenly clear. Mr Closer's behaviour was pre-arranged. Mr Closer had given an undertaking to his daughter, Hannah Closer, not to interfere in any way with her eighteenth birthday celebrations, regardless of what ravages the guests inflicted. His one condition was that he should retain the right to be a silent witness, to look on while his house was destroyed. This was the meaning of the mordant, suffering light in his eye. His non-intervention was his birthday gift to his much-loved daughter.

God knows what time.

I ONCE did have a long talk with Mr Closer, in fact – about 'go', the Japanese board game. It turned out that he was a great go player.

The occasion was shortly after the incident with the kite, but before the party. I had gone to the Closer residence one evening to see Dr Closer, but Mr Closer answered the door and informed me that Dr Closer was out. Mr Closer said that Dr Closer would be back soon, and asked me if I would like to come in and have a cup of tea. It was a rather long way back to Winterbank from the Closer residence, so I accepted his offer.

Mr Closer sat me down and gave me a cigarette. I should say that although I don't smoke now, I did occasionally have a cigarette in those days. My encounter with pleurisy means that smoking is now quite uncomfortable.

Mr Closer sat himself down, and began, without much in the way of preamble, to talk about go. The house was quite dark. The front room, where we were sitting, was lit by a single lamp.

Mr Closer's line of talk soon proved quite difficult to follow. I had – and still have – only the most basic grasp of go, and Mr Closer's conversation seemed to revolve chiefly around the latest developments in go *computing*. Therefore his talk was in effect not of one, but of two arcane fields: go and computing. I found after the first ten minutes that I had nothing whatever to contribute; and the conversation, which even to begin with had been a rather one-sided affair, frankly turned into a lecture. As it washed over me, I found I was smoking cigarette after cigarette, not because I wanted to, but just to have something to do.

Quite soon I began to feel sick. It was chiefly the cigarettes; but the strain of listening to Mr Closer – who really and truly seemed to think I understood him – was also a factor. Every now and then he would interrupt himself with a sly look at me and a 'you see?', but I could hardly respond in the negative, since this would certainly have elicited a series of further lengthy explanations which I would then also fail to understand. So I simply nodded. I was being buried deeper and deeper in an avalanche of words, and I wanted urgently to escape. If I could manage at least some small remark that showed I had a glimmer of comprehension of what he had been saying, then perhaps I could stand and leave; if I could say *something* – even just one sentence – then I could get away with a shred of dignity intact! But in fact I could think of nothing, absolutely nothing to say, and felt sicker and sicker with every passing moment.

At length the situation became desperate. Mr Closer showed no sign of reaching any conclusion. I felt strongly that I wanted to vomit. In fact, I knew that if I didn't leave immediately I would vomit there and then, on the floor, in front of him – and that the mess at his feet would be my only comment. I could feel my stomach beginning to contract. I knew I had only a matter of seconds before I voided the filthy cigarettes onto his shoes.

I rose without uttering a word, my head reeling. 'Sorry, I have to go,' I blurted out. I ran for the door.

Mr Closer also rose, a look of puzzlement on his face. He followed behind me into the hall. 'All right then, see you!' he called, but I was already sprinting down the path. I heard the front door snap shut behind me.

Immediately I lurched into the bushes in the driveway and emptied the contents of my stomach.

When I had finished, I cleaned my mouth as best I could and began staggering homewards. I was quite sure – rather irrationally, with the benefit of hindsight – that he had planned the whole thing. I suspected too that he had heard me vomiting into his bushes.

Then at the end of the driveway I saw Hannah. Dr Closer wasn't with her.

Hannah, it seemed, was weeping. She saw me coming towards her, but didn't try to wipe the tears from her eyes. Even though I had myself recently had a bruising encounter, I was dumbstruck. Why was she in tears? Who had hurt her? I wanted very much to approach her, to comfort her, but felt terribly ashamed. Perhaps Hannah had heard me vomiting, and perhaps, in fact – horrible to think – there were still flecks of vomit on my clothing or on my mouth.

'What's the matter?' I asked her.

'I was on the bus,' she said, 'and I started thinking about *Away in a Manger.*'

Of course. The carol *was* moving: the little Lord Jesus, with no crib for a bed, worshipped by gentle farm animals and shepherds, simple folk who were prepared to kneel and adore the Christ-child.

But I could find nothing to say.

'Bye, Nicholas,' Hannah said, and walked home up the driveway.

As above.

HOWEVER, I haven't really finished telling you about the party.

By the time it ended, the house was in a state of some chaos. I say it 'ended', but the majority of the guests had not actually left. Instead they had simply dropped to the floor and begun sleeping. The house, as I have said, was on the outskirts of Hull, perhaps two miles from the city; and although this was not so very far to walk, many of the guests had obviously not wished to go on foot all that way late at night. So they had simply settled themselves on the floor, just like that, with no bedclothes. There were at least a hundred people there, sleeping like seals. Or, if they weren't sleeping, they were at least lying down. It was all remarkably civilized. 'Garg' was there, now I come to think of it.

I too tried to sleep, but my head was full of thoughts of Madeleine. I had seen Madeline briefly, earlier on, her boots flashing as she ran up the stairs, but I hadn't followed her. And now that everyone had decided to go to sleep, I wanted to find her. All I wished for, girls, was to have a quick chat with her. The thing was, I had no idea where she was sleeping. I got up and began searching for her. This was quite ambitious in the circumstances, since I was drunk, and it was dark, and the house was enormous.

In my addled state, I determined to search every inch of the house. I began with the reception area, stumbling around, peering at the recumbent forms; I then checked the kitchen and the various bathrooms and workrooms; I moved to the dining-room, and then the sitting room, which, perhaps because of the soft furnishings and thick carpets, was crammed full. I soon found that the best method of locomotion was to crawl, peering at the faces. Madeleine was nowhere to be seen. I decided therefore to turn my attention to the upper rooms.

There were two upper floors, with five or six rooms each. The first-floor bedrooms were, not unsurprisingly, all full: there were couples, threesomes or foursomes in each bed, and more on the floor or on divans or chairs. Some were asleep in the en-suite bathrooms, some in the baths themselves. In each room was the murmur of breathing bodies, and occasionally the cry of a dreamer. There was no sign of Madeleine. So I made my way to the little staircase to the second floor. Here I encountered an obstruction. The staircase had been shut off by a door, which had been locked. The family, I thought, must be up there. They had reserved that floor for their use. Dr Closer and Mr Closer, as well as Hannah Closer, were up there. They had, as it were, barricaded themselves off from the rest of the guests, not unreasonably. I will admit I was a little annoyed at that, since it prevented me from searching the entire house as I had planned. However, Madeleine was highly unlikely to be up there; and short of breaking the door down there was nothing to be done. I had now exhausted all avenues. Was it possible Madeleine had left the party? Who could have given her a lift? Should I walk home now? I didn't really want to wake the following morning, alone, at the Closer residence. Perhaps if I walked back to her rooms in Polder Row I would see her light on. Though this wasn't likely, since by the time I got there, Madeleine would long since have gone to bed.

I must have been standing by the door to the little staircase, thinking, when a ghostly figure loomed up out of the dark. It was Mr Closer.

'Aren't you asleep?' he asked. 'It's Nicholas, isn't it?'

I replied that it was.

'Do you want to go to sleep?' Mr Closer asked. 'I think there's some space downstairs.'

'No, thanks,' I said.

'Well, you can't stay like that all night,' Mr Closer said. 'Come along, come downstairs.'

'But you must not intervene,' I said.

'I beg your pardon?' His shirt looked purple in the gloom.

'You promised,' I told him, 'that you would not.'

Mr Closer now came a little closer. I saw his expression of quick, ironic intelligence. He was obviously completely sober. I saw also that that he held a key.

'Yes,' he said slowly.

'Do you know why you and I are still awake,' I asked him, 'when everyone else is asleep?'

'No,' Mr Closer said, smiling a little.

'For love,' I said.

About 10 pm.

I AM feeling a little feverish. It's possible that the rain has had some effect on me. This cell is rather poorly heated. We've now been here for around eleven hours. The young man with the Elvis tattoo has been taken away, so I have got his bunk, which fortunately has blankets. 'Beaver' and I talked a little, but now he is asleep. Next door someone was making a loud noise. It seemed a bit early for a drunk. Then it struck me that it was most likely Tim, the ex-doctor.

As above.

AFTER THAT conversation in the small hours with Mr Closer I walked home.

The night was warm and there was a dull orange moon. My way home went by Pearson Park. Philip Larkin's house was on the fringes of this particular park – as I think I have mentioned – as was the shared house of Aurora. Both were well known to most of the students. I made my way into the park and sat on a seesaw, from which I had a good view of the Larkin residence. I was quite familiar with its outlines. It was a slightly eerie building: it reminded me of a long tooth. All the lights in the tooth were out. Was Larkin in there, asleep, at that very moment? What would he do if I rang the bell? What would he say? All sorts of strange ideas went through my mind. I was still, I think, a little dissatisfied with my encounter with Larkin at the university, and felt that I should have said something more to him. Unfortunately, even now, twenty-eight years later, I still have no idea what I could have said, in the middle of a deserted university, at night... What *do* you say in that situation?

I didn't feel in the least tired. I got up from the seesaw and went to sit on the wall of a little pond. I imagined what it would be like to be a boy again, playing with a boat. The pond shimmered in the silence. Reeds and bulrushes had choked two thirds of it. I wondered where Madeleine was, and felt, as I often did then, in a curious state of limbo. My parents were dead; there was no need to look for work; I rarely went out, didn't eat much, had no expensive hobbies; all I did was read and scribble. That, girls, was the sum total of my life. It was a couple of years before the opening of the Institute. My understanding with Madeleine was at an end: Madeleine would shortly graduate, and have a job; meanwhile I was not even a student. I was nothing, really – just a scribbler, hanging around aimlessly, waiting. A member of the last generation.

The bulrushes scraped together with a dry sound. It was the 'Indian summer', so called, but decay had already set in, turning everything brown and dry. I really had no sense of life continuing for more than a matter of a few days or weeks. The planets would shortly be in alignment, then missiles would descend and burn everything up. London, Birmingham, Leeds, Glasgow, Hull. This little park would go, of course – the little pond would dry up in a flash, the bulrushes exploding, the trees vaporizing. Like me, the park was just waiting around for the end. But natural things accept death. It was really only the humans who were out of place.

I hoped my own death would not be too painful.

I got up from the edge of the pond and walked toward the Larkin house, still in darkness.

Then, as I reached the pavement, I noticed a figure near me. I recognized Henry, the young man who had taken his clothes off in the little dining-room with the iguanodon. It was not altogether surprising to see Henry there. Pearson Park was not so very far away from the shared house in Christiania Street; moreover, as I have said, it was the location of the shared house of Aurora.

Henry's face seemed green. 'Larkin's asleep,' he said, pointing up at the house.

'What are you doing?' I asked.

Henry took an envelope from his back pocket. He

held it up, grinning in a strange manner. 'Posting a letter,' he said.

'It doesn't have a stamp,' I said.

'No – I'm going to deliver it by hand. It's for Aurora.'

Henry, it seemed, had fallen in love. I had suspected it for some time, and now here was the confirmation. Henry was quite a confident young man – he was quite capable of taking his clothes off in a roomful of people, for example – but, in the presence of Aurora, his manner always seemed a little strained; he was liable to talk loudly and make jokes that were not funny. This made his feelings plain for all to see. As for the letter, Henry wasn't in the habit of writing letters to any of his girlfriends. He was more generally the recipient of letters.

'Of course, there's no point in putting things off,' Henry continued, regarding me critically, 'but even so... I've been standing here since midnight. I can't quite bring myself to do it.'

'What does it say?' I asked.

Henry thrust it at me. 'Read it.'

The envelope was unsealed. I retrieved the note inside.

'Dear Aurora,' it read. 'I must tell you that I am in love with you. You may well protest that I don't really know you and therefore I can't be. I would reply that this isn't the case, and that if you knew how much I loved you, you wouldn't say that. Meet me at the Little Alex tomorrow night (Sunday) at nine pm. Love Henry.'

I passed it back to him, intending to comment, when a light snapped on in Larkin's bathroom. Henry saw it too. We both stopped what we were doing: I was still holding the letter out to Henry. A figure was clearly silhouetted in the window. It was certainly not Larkin. It was a woman: a young woman, quite petite, with an oval face and hair cut short at nape-length. Then the light snapped off.

•

Was it Aurora at the window? It seems highly unlikely. First, there is no mention of Aurora in any of the biographies of Larkin, nor in any of his letters. If Larkin had been involved with Aurora he would surely have mentioned it in a letter to Kingsley Amis. Second, Aurora never, in my hearing at least, mentioned Larkin, and there was never any gossip concerning Aurora and Larkin. Third, Larkin was fifty-nine years old at the time, and Aurora was nineteen. However, none of this takes into account the fact that there was *a young woman at the window, even if it was not Aurora. Neither does it take into account the fact that Aurora could easily have been on friendly terms with Larkin, since she was his neighbour in Pearson Park.*

And finally, neither does it take into account the fact that stranger things have happened – as Yeats pointed out.

Henry, I think, was of the opinion that it was Aurora at the window. However, he didn't say anything. He simply crumpled up the letter. I think he was about to throw it to the ground when he changed his mind and put it in his pocket. Then he walked away without a word.

Shortly afterwards I too left the park and went home. It was four o'clock in the morning and the first glimmers of dawn were beginning to show over the roofs.

As above.

Apropos OF Aurora I must just relate an incident which occurred some time during my first year at Hull. I and a friend had spent the evening at a pub called the Little Alex – the very one Henry had mentioned in his note to Aurora – and had become quite drunk. I'm afraid we were always doing that in those days, girls. For some reason we conceived the plan of going over to Aurora's house in Pearson Park. I can't now remember what we expected to do once we got there. To pay our respects, probably. So this friend and I – it was actually the young man whose name I can't remember – walked the half-mile or so to Aurora's. Once there, we didn't call straight away, but instead went into the little back garden. We were now right underneath Aurora's window; her room, as I think I mentioned earlier, was on the first floor, at the back. From our vantage point in the garden we could see a light on in her room. It was about eleven-thirty at night.

It was at this point that the young man whose name I can't remember suggested that we approach Aurora's window by *climbing* up to it. As it happened, in the garden was an old wooden ladder with grass growing through it. I agreed that it might be fun. I think perhaps I was too drunk to assess the situation properly. No sooner had the plan been mentioned than the young man was excitedly wresting the ladder from the lawn – he had to tear it from the earth, almost, leaving bare patches. I then helped him carry it, still half covered in vegetation, to the window.

The young man whose name I can't remember suggested that I should be the one to climb, since I knew Aurora better than he. I agreed. I began climbing, though quite gingerly, because the ladder was very old. Soon I had reached the sill. I looked in at the window. And there –

But perhaps I really shouldn't describe what I saw. Aurora herself saw me and regarded me quite calmly.

From below I heard the sound of laughter. It is still a little painful, even now, to think about it.

·

Unfortunately that will have to be cut.

·

Where is Aurora now, I wonder? Is it really possible she is forty-seven years old?

As above.

I AM beginning to feel quite hot and strange, though at the same time cold and shivery. I have obviously contracted a mild fever. This is the worst sort of place to become ill – a cell – especially if one doesn't have one's own clothes, and is dressed only in a blanket. What's more, my pills are in my jacket. When we arrived I decided not to tell the guard about them. I suppose I thought that I could survive well enough without them. This is a very bad habit of mine: I continually impute to myself powers of endurance that are entirely imaginary. And now without the pills I am beginning to feel extremely nervous.

As above.

I REMEMBER another funny thing that happened to do with the Little Alex. Give me a moment and I will remember it.

·

Actually, it's quite impossible. Alice... Oh God, it's too disgusting. No. I really can't bear to think about it.

As above.

THEY HAVE taken 'Beaver' out of the cell. Where they are taking him, I have no idea. It is very late for a release. Shortly after he left, I heard the cell two doors down being opened, and then, soon afterwards, banged shut. This seemed a good sign: the cell two doors down is I think the one that holds Tim, the ex-doctor. So perhaps he too is being discharged.

·

Imagine my astonishment! Five minutes after writing the above I heard the voice of 'Beaver', quite plainly, calling the guard to let him go to the toilet! And then 'Beaver' walked past my cell! He even waved to me! It was clear that 'Beaver' had merely been moved from the cell, and not released at all. That was the meaning of the cell door being opened and shut. Why on earth had they done this? I am utterly perplexed. Had they moved 'Beaver' to go in with Tim because Tim had requested it? Or were they worried for the health or welfare of Tim in some way, and decided he needed a companion?

In prison you feel almost like a child. What the authorities do is incomprehensible and must simply be accepted. Like a child, you must ask to go to the toilet, must depend on the authorities for a favour or a kind word, and are in fact utterly at the mercy of those whose duty it is to care for you.

So now I am alone. I am sitting up in bed scribbling this. Actually, I don't feel too bad.

As above.

HENRY DID confront Aurora on the matter of Larkin, I remember. It was a few days after Henry and I had seen the figure of a young woman at Larkin's window.

Aurora was at the house in Christiania Street – she didn't often call, but had come, I think, to visit Lara (of whom I still haven't told you anything) – and was standing in the small dining room. I was visiting the young man whose name I can't remember, for something to do: I was hoping, I think, that Madeleine might be there, but she was out.

Aurora looked rather out of place in the shared house in Christiania Street. Aurora never wore the damp woollen clothing common to most of the young women of my acquaintance. On this occasion she was dressed in spotless cream trousers, with a cream silk blouse that set off her dark hair very well, and a silver torque. She looked very beautiful. Lara was talking to her about something or other – I will get around to describing Lara in a moment – when suddenly Henry burst into the room. He looked very flushed and unhappy. Henry, despite his general confidence with young women and tendency to take his clothes off, was now behaving very oddly. Aurora, however, didn't greet him or even look at him directly; instead, an expression of mild irritation passed across her face. I guessed that something disagreeable had already occurred between them.

'I wanted to talk to you,' Henry said, rudely interrupting Lara.

Aurora raised her eyebrows.

'But not here,' Henry went on.

'Why not?' asked Aurora.

'Privately.'

'I'm afraid I don't have time...' Aurora began, but Henry stopped her by reaching out and touching her on the shoulder, on her silk blouse. It was only a light touch, with one finger, but a world of terrible longing was compressed into it. Aurora recoiled, a look of very great displeasure on her face.

'I saw you in the house of our poet,' Henry said.

'What?' Aurora said.

'Larkin,' said Henry.

Aurora said nothing.

'You don't deny it, then?'

'Deny what?'

'That you were at Larkin's house.'

'Where I go is none of your business.'

Aurora turned back to talk to Lara. Henry had said his piece, and now stood there breathing heavily. He had conducted his investigation with a very great lack of skill. In the space of a few seconds he had made himself *persona non grata*, and gained nothing in the way of information. Presumably we would never know, now, whether it had been Aurora at Larkin's.

It seemed that Henry was unable to move; he just continued standing there in front of her, breathing like a bullock. Even his curly hair seemed defeated. Aurora knew full well, as did anyone else who cared to enquire, that Henry was terribly love with her – it was written all over him – but she cared not a whit.

Suddenly Henry grabbed Aurora. He took her shoulders with both hands and thrust his face into hers, trying to kiss her. Aurora threw back her head, and Henry missed her mouth by several inches. There was a painful collision. Aurora gave a cry and pushed Henry off. She put her hand to her mouth, which had struck his forehead. Henry, appalled by what he had done, and still unable to speak, continued standing in front of her, his face contorted, his hands working in the air.

Just at that moment Lara kicked Henry very hard in the groin.

•

It is only now that I realise that the business of being kicked in the groin is something of a leitmotif. *I hadn't realised, I think, how prevalent this was in the 1980s. Certainly you don't hear very much about its being done now. Besides, young women today do not wear the same sort of footwear.*

I should add that groin-kicking tended to be a defensive measure only. Once their man was down there was never any attempt to continue the punishment. One kick was generally enough.

I find myself at a slight disadvantage here: I do not at all wish to suggest to the girls that kicking young men in the groin is a reasonable way to behave, to resolve disputes. Therefore I should flag this episode.

However, I can't really leave it out. If I do, nothing I have said makes sense.

•

What happened next was rather confused. Aurora and Lara left the dining room to go upstairs to Lara's attic. Shortly afterwards, Aurora left the house. I didn't see either of them again that evening. I stayed instead with Henry in the dining room with the iguanodon.

After a while he picked himself up from the floor and sat in an armchair. He was weeping.

'Do you think it was her?' he asked me after a time.

'I don't know,' I said.

As above.

I looked at my hand just now as it held the pen. It looked old. I stopped writing and stretched it out to examine it more closely. It seemed to have aged twenty years in the last few hours. It looked the way I remember my grandfather's hands looking when I was a child. Something about those hands, the hands of my grandfather, always disturbed me. The skin did not seem to belong to them, but instead seemed to have been wrapped onto them like the bandages of a mummy. And there were lots of blue-black marks where they had been knocked, just in the course of everyday use. Now my own hands look like that. How did they get so old, so quickly? Who would wish to be touched by them? It would be like submitting to the caresses of a mummy! And my face? I don't have a mirror in here, but if I did, what would it look like? Surely not like these hands! Oh! What's wrong with me? Shrouded in a blanket, in my underpants... Why am I here? Of course I know the answer to that – but I'm too old for this sort of thing – I've got to get out of here! Really...! This is no way to carry on. I need clothes! Eating Sunday lunch in soaking underpants...? Why haven't they brought me my clothes? They must be dry by now! Is everyone asleep? This light! It's buzzing!

Only Alice would look at me now. Alice, who refused to distinguish between people on the basis of their personal appearance... poor dead Alice... would she allow herself to be caressed by these hands? Perhaps that would be too much even for her... but of course there's no hope of that... Alice is long dead...

•

I went to Alice's funeral, actually. I managed to get some time off from the Institute. I wept throughout. Her mother was there, and insisted that Alice was still alive, in the spiritual realm, and that Alice was still in touch with her. Her mother claimed, in fact, that Alice visited her, and had visited her that very morning, the morning of the funeral. She had not visited in person: she had visited instead in the form of an aroma, the aroma of flowers.

Alice's funeral was in Great Yarmouth, where she had grown up. Before the service I spent some time traipsing about the streets, particularly along the sea-front. I went into a junk shop and bought something very silly – a large portrait of a lady, which was later quite difficult to manage on the train. I must have been very drunk and maudlin, because at the first pub I went into I asked the barman: 'Do you know a young woman called Alice? She used to live here. I think she used to come into this pub' (although I had no idea whether or not this was the case). The barman, a young man of twenty or so, shook his head, eyeing me carefully. 'No,' he said. To him I was an old man. Did he guess what was going through my mind? If Alice had been any friend of mine that would make her, in all likelihood, an old woman. He could never have known her when she was at large in Great Yarmouth, rampaging around, in her teenage years, before coming to university… So he said 'no', and continued polishing his glass. Did he sense the maudlin futility of my question? There are, of course, a million Alices. The barman knew, I think, that my question was not a real request for information, and that what I was really asking him was as follows: 'Do you realise, sir, that a person exists for a short time, then dies and is forgotten? Or to put it another way, that first there is a person who is known to everyone, whose name is on everyone's lips, whose face is fresh and lovely, whose cheeks are pink, whose eyes are delicate and a little mischievous, whose eyelashes quiver demurely on her milk-white skin, who is so full of life that it seems as if death will, for once, fail in his purposes? But that this person, sir, is in fact as vulnerable as everyone else, and can be taken over by all the ravages of time, and utterly destroyed? For the true enemy of man is not death, but life! Life is the destroyer, and death merely the dustman. And even that is not all! For when life has done its dirty business and death has dragged away the corpse for disposal, the final eradication begins: memories in human skulls begin to atrophy, documents are lost or thrown away, friends and family die, and finally nothing is left at all except perhaps an unregarded headstone, which is then in its turn kicked over or crumbles to dust.' Of course the barman, a lad of twenty, knew all this, since lads of twenty are long familiar with these tropes of decay and death: this was why he hadn't said anything, or had restricted himself to the single syllable 'no'. Even if he didn't know it he could soon infer it from my withered hands and the deep shadows under my eyes. He had seen at once that I did not wish to ask about Alice, what she looked like, how old she was, whose friend she was, but about myself... My actual question, he had seen, with quick insight, was symbolic...

Alice. After her annihilating splash she was swept out into the ocean, where she became a piece of trash to be picked at by fish, succumbing in the end to the pull of the seabed, where her bones lay scattered and melting into the sand.

Difficult to tell: about one o'clock in the morning?

HANNAH KNEW everything, of course, even when she met me on the path with the tears streaming down her face. This would have been in the October of 1982, the month when the planets were all in alignment. A few days after her eighteenth birthday party, I bumped into her in the public library. Hannah told me that her parents were about to get divorced.

'Why?' I asked.

Hannah gave me a level stare. 'My mother,' she said, 'has got someone else.'

I immediately thought of Madeleine. 'Who?' I asked.

'Your friend Madeleine,' she replied.

I blundered out of the library, crossed the main street and went into a telephone box, where I called for a taxi. Of course, this was in the days before mobile phones. Just as the taxi was arriving, Hannah also ran out of the library, waved at me, crossed the road, and got into the cab next to me, as I had done when Madeleine had taken the cab to see the Asian man.

She began crying. I asked if she had a handkerchief, and she said no. Unfortunately I had none of my own to offer her. I wanted to stroke her hair, but felt that there would be time for that in the future, when I was not in love with Madeleine.

Five minutes later the cab was crunching up the drive of the Closer residence. I paid the driver, and we got out. Hannah opened the front door with her key and we walked into the kitchen.

•

Sitting at the table, as I guessed there would be, were Madeleine, Dr Closer and Mr Closer. On the table was a large bottle of wine, the sort that one might bring back from a foreign holiday. It was half drunk.

Mr Closer gestured broadly at Madeleine and Dr Closer. 'We're negotiating,' he said, slurring his words slightly. 'Please join us.' Then he got up and left the room.

I advanced to the kitchen table: Hannah stood behind me in the doorway. Madeleine seemed a little annoyed. Dr Closer's face as she looked at me bore an expression of tenderness.

'Are you in love?' I asked Madeleine.

I suppose at this moment it will be expected that Madeleine got up from the table and kicked me in the groin; or that Dr Closer did so; or that Hannah kicked her own mother in the groin; or some such permutation. However, nothing of the sort happened. Dr Closer didn't say anything, and Hannah remained silent, in the doorway. It was Madeleine who spoke.

'Caroline and I want to be together, Nicholas,' she said.

'Nicholas…' began Dr Closer, half rising and reaching out to me. But I felt the powerful desire to vomit. Near the kitchen was the half-open door of the bathroom: I scuttled for it as fast as I could. The vomit had already appeared in my mouth as I reached the door, and it was only by sheer luck that I didn't make more of a mess.

•

By the way, I don't blame Hannah for anything. Why should I? She was always so kind to me. I remember one morning, before I was due to take a test, she gave me something she had drawn. It was a cartoon strip based on the story 'The Nose' by Nikolai Gogol. Perhaps it was the coincidence of my own name – Nicholas – with Gogol's that inspired her. Anyway, the cartoon was very funny. It depicted the Nose going into an examination room to take *a test: the Nose made its way to a desk, took a pen in its hand, and began to write. I don't remember how it ended, or indeed whether it did end — it was only three frames long, I think. But I remember Hannah's face as she handed it to me, from her mother's Wolseley. She looked sad.*

Anyone looking at the situation from the outside would conclude that you were in love with me, Hannah.

Oh girls, girls, what a foolish old man your father is. And how wonderful it is that all this suffering finally came to an end. After all, first the Institute came along, and then you arrived. Actually I seem to have forgotten what I am doing, because this part should not be in italics, but in roman. No matter. I'll edit it all later.

As above.

FIRST THE young man with the Elvis tattoo vanished, and then 'Beaver', leaving me all alone. And now night has descended, deeply, darkly: no stars are visible. It is cold. When will I be released? Come to think of it, I haven't even had any dinner... Oh yes, wait – it was lasagna. Is it perhaps earlier than I think? Why hasn't anybody been in to tell me what's going on?

But I have only been here a few hours, so I mustn't fuss. If I start pleading my case with them now, they'll just laugh – I've only been here a few hours! I certainly can't crack now. But it is very difficult, girls, to maintain one's equilibrium in a place such as this, with no clothes on, when one is forced to stay under the blankets just to keep warm, when one is hungry and unfed... Only the writing of this journal is keeping me going. Otherwise I find my mind beginning to drift.

As above.

I

THROUGH

THESE

GIRLS,

THE

THROUGH

THE

LEAVES

A

FORGOTTEN

A

A

SUMMER

PICNIC.

Two in the morning by Madeleine's watch.

YOU WON'T believe this, girls, but Madeleine herself just walked into this cell. She was real, absolutely real. She had joined the police after all. She was older, of course, but still quite recognizable. She was in police uniform.

Madeleine no longer looked as she had done when we shared the same house together, in Christiania Street, so long, long ago. She now wore make-up, which she had never done before. There were lines on her face that hadn't been there, especially around the mouth. She had also cut her hair, and it seemed to have less volume.

'Nicholas,' she said. She was standing in the cell doorway holding some keys. 'What have they done to you?'

I couldn't at first reply. Why had she put it quite like that? Was it because I was wrapped in a blanket, and hadn't washed or shaved for a day, and my hair was sticking up? Or because I was now forty-eight?

'Madeleine...' I stammered. 'You joined the police, then.'

She advanced into the cell. 'I saw your name in the book,' she said. 'I thought it must be you. How are you?'

'I'm fine,' I said. 'How are you?'

'I'm fine,' she said. 'I'm married now. I've got two girls. One eight and one ten. Katy and Amy. What about you? You're still living in Hull, aren't you?'

'Yes.'

'And still... in that place?'

'You really ought to come to the Institute,' I said. 'We do a lot of good work.'

'Yes, I might do that.' Madeleine sat next to me on the bunk. She had put on weight. All of a sudden I didn't love her any more.

'But really, Nicholas,' she went on, 'you must try to get out of that place. Really. You used to be so clever. You were studying Chinese. I can't believe you've spent all these years cooped up in there.'

I didn't reply.

Madeleine fished into one of the many pockets in her tunic and brought out a small bottle of pills.

'I got you these,' she said. 'We found them in your clothes.' She handed me the bottle. 'I looked them up. I hope you don't mind. Your clothes were so wet that we missed them. You really should be taking them.'

Then Madeleine gently took back the bottle she had just given me – rather as the policeman had taken back the letter I'd sent to my MP – opened it, and shook three pills into her hand. 'I'll give you three,' she said. 'One for now, two for later. Do you want some water?'

'No thanks,' I said.

Madeleine put the bottle back into her pocket. 'We'll be letting you go in the morning. I'm sorry it's taking so long.' She smiled sadly. 'But really, Nicholas, why are you still doing all this? You really shouldn't be getting involved in this sort of thing. I think they're taking advantage of you.'

I felt a reflex of anger rising in me. I wanted to tell Madeleine that there could hardly be anything more important than a threat to the entire world; that it was the duty of every citizen to protest against the crimes of his or her own government; and that many of the most distinguished people, such as Bertrand Russell, had been prisoners of conscience. But then I remembered that I no longer loved her, and that she was married with two girls.

'I'm sorry I can't stay,' she said. 'We're really busy

at the moment. I know it's two o'clock but this is our busiest time… I'll come and check on you later.' She stood up. 'Try to get some sleep. I'll see you aren't disturbed.'

'Madeleine,' I said, as she reached the door. 'Are you still a vegetarian?'

She gave a small smile, and for a moment looked the way I remembered.

'I try to be,' she said.

She walked out, and immediately I fell asleep. I had a very bad dream. Madeleine and I – the old Madeleine – were trying to teach one of our girls to cross the road. I think it was Amy. Amy said that she could do it, but obviously she was not yet at that age when she was able to take sufficient care. She didn't look from side to side properly. But she made it safely across. I asked her to come back and then do it again, this time making Madeleine watch, to show Madeleine, in fact, that Amy couldn't really do it on her own, and that it was a little too early to trust her. It was a main road, after all, not a little side street. Why were we letting Amy practice on such a busy road? I have no idea. In any case, Amy stepped out into the road, where the traffic was so heavy that one lane – the nearest – was at a standstill, but instead of negotiating her way through the cars she sat down on the front bumper of a large truck. Just sat down on it, I suppose for a joke. But the driver didn't see that she had done this – he was too high up – and just drove off with her still sitting on the bumper. I ran after the truck in panic. At any moment she might hop off and be killed. I ran after the truck, but it had disappeared. I was no longer even sure what colour the truck was or even whether it had been a truck or a car. I ran back to Madeleine and told her I hadn't found the vehicle in question. She was distraught. I told her that Amy must be all right or we'd have heard something. We discussed in the garden what to do. Madeleine was weeping. We went upstairs. It was a Tudor bedroom. We looked through the windows out onto the road. We had the strong feeling that if there'd been an accident of any kind, the traffic, which was heavy, would be utterly jammed; we'd hear police and ambulance sirens; but everything seemed to be running as normal. Everything, therefore, was going to be all right. But I don't think I believed it, and nor did I care particularly. Then we both saw something. I think we both saw it at the same time. Oh, God! It was disgusting. No... no... I can barely bring myself to write it down... her body was there, in the road... oh... oh, I feel sick... the cars were just driving over and over her...

·

A dream is only a dream, of course. Still, it had quite an effect on me. Now, in this lonely cave in the Highlands, my girls seem very remote. It seems unlikely that I will ever see them again. Their existence is now like a dim torch, with batteries that are fading, fading... I can't picture their faces as I used to.

Close to dawn.

I AM slightly worried about getting the coach back to Hull. I'm sure Guy and the others will have been released by now. Guy has lovers in the police, as everyone knows. No one minds. We accept her little peculiarities because she does such sterling work.

The way they take fingerprints in here is very strange. The patient is laid out on a wide table and rolled over and over like a rolling pin, by policewomen in floury aprons. When the soul has made a good impression, the pastry is taken off and stored in special drawers. At a later date, after the patient's death, it is weighed. The way they do this is interesting. They weigh it against a feather. If the soul is heavier, the verdict is 'guilty'. If lighter, the verdict is 'innocent'.

Is that you, Guy? And what do you mean by an 'epithet' to my diary? Do you mean you want to write an 'epitaph'? Are you a dream? Yes… of course you are. But you seem very real, standing there. You must mean an epitaph. If you were to write an 'epithet' to my diary it would be something such as 'Nicholas is an idiot': that is what would appear on the title page. But even so, you yourself cannot write an epitaph. You have to suggest a quotation, perhaps from a famous author, or, in your case, authoress. Or will you choose a man's words? But what man has ever said anything worth quoting?

Now you are here, Guy, though only in the form of a wraith – I am still quite sane enough to know that you are a hallucination – I am not scared of you. I hope your lovers appreciate you, Guy.

Oh, what a vile thing to say.

But don't you know I am only a man? Can you not find it in yourself to forgive us, as a sex? Men create wars, that's true... we have a lot to answer for. Perhaps we should hang our heads in shame. But why shouldn't we look at a woman's breasts? They are only bags of fat... And now I see that I didn't mean 'epitaph', I meant 'epigraph'. So, Guy, would you like to suggest an epigraph? Perhaps something from one of the great female writers: Madame Bovary, for example? No, no, Madame Bovary wasn't a writer: she was a fictional character. She was also an adulteress: she betrayed her husband on at least two occasions, with different men, in a coach. But she was more sinned against than sinning. The men in her life were equally to blame. Take her husband, Charles. He was futile and weak.

You're not speaking, Guy. And your voice would be so comforting – like warm honey. Come closer. No? You prefer to stand there, twisting and untwisting your hair? Do you want a cup of hot water? What hope is there for the world, Guy? Will nuclear weapons ever be abolished? Come closer. You, I am sure, would advocate a healthy and harmonious sex life.

Such long hair. But you haven't suggested an epigraph, preferring perhaps your original suggestion, an epithet. And now I see that 'epithet' was what you meant all along. How stupid I am! I missed the most important criterion. I should have trusted you. So what is your 'epithet'? How will you characterize me? Actually, I am all of a sudden very interested. Tell me what you think of me. Don't hold back, and don't worry if it is negative: I can take it. I know at least that it will be fair. I trust you. I know that there will not be a shred of maliciousness in it, Guy, because you are a good person.

Yes, I should learn something today…

Oh, you are fading. Oh, well. That's it, then. I think I knew, deep down, that you would never tell me. You are fading, without saying goodbye. I can still see your eyes… you look irritated… I hope they let you out soon.

See you in the coach, Madame?

•

I now feel a little clearer in my mind. These hallucinations are quite normal when I don't take my pills regularly. They come in fits and starts. Now I feel quite normal. I still haven't taken the pills that Madeleine gave me. Why bother? Am I to spend the rest of my life taking pills?

I have reviewed what I have written above and I am afraid that this diary has broken down almost beyond recall. It will need to be severely edited when I get home: the blue pencil will come out with a vengeance. Luckily I am a good editor. I ruthlessly murder my best phrases.

Just now, while I dozed, I had another terrible dream. Why don't I ever have any nice dreams? It was about Madeleine again. In the dream I learned that Madeleine had died. I got a letter from her most recent Italian boyfriend, who seemed a wry and worldly fellow. He interspersed his sentences with Latin comments. 'So you bedded her,' he began. 'I too tasted her body, I too plunged into her. Miserere nobis. *She was lost at sea. A flare was sent up. She was never found. She is 'missing'. Here is the transcript of the radio operator. It is the only document. She is dead. At the theatre she would always seem more interested in the leading man than in anything I ever said.* Requiescat in pace.'

Oh, what a disgusting dream.

•

Thank you so much for coming. It's wonderful to see you – you haven't changed a bit. Of course, that's to be expected from a hallucination. But in a sense you are quite real. Whatever you say or do will be completely unexpected, just as in real life.

I may never get another chance to tell you this, Hannah dear – don't go up and down like that, you're making me feel sick – but I have always loved you. Your heart was always so pure, and your beauty so golden. Can someone love two girls at the same time? Yes, yes, absolutely yes! Just as one can love and hate at the same time! But don't bring your mother here. I don't think I could bear to see her.

Oh!

Your mother told you to appear in your underwear to make me fall in love with you so she could have Madeleine?

No, no, Hannah, it's not true!

Don't say it!

I won't hear it! Girls! Leave the cell now! No, that is disgusting! I won't hear it! I don't believe it! What mother would prostitute her daughter in that way? And you, Hannah, you went along with it? How could you? I am disgusted with both of you! Get out of my sight! Go, go, go! Go to your lovers! Did you treat them all as heartlessly as you treated me?

You are no longer young, Hannah, you are an old woman. Perhaps your mother is dead now. She was forty-seven then, and now she is seventy. Can she still speak Chinese? Oh God, I want to vomit. Guard, bring a bucket!

•

How odd. Lara. And the girls know nothing about you.

They wouldn't know, for example, that you were a singer in your own group. You never stood at the front of the stage, as is usual. You crouched somewhere towards the back. Your rationale in so doing, I assumed, was that no member of the group should have prominence over any other.

Yes... the 1980s were a very strange time. For example, I remember one afternoon going to the cafeteria and seeing a strange notice on the door. Unfortunately I can't remember the exact wording, but it was *something* such as the following:

A few
W O M Y N
will discuss their work
1.00 pm in the canteen
all W O M Y N welcome.

How strange! I remember looking at it for a long time trying to work it out. 'Womyn': was it pronounced the same as 'Women' or was this an entirely new sex? And looking through the doors the whole cafeteria had been taken over by young women from the arts and architecture faculty. 'A few'!? They were like ants! I knew I would never get in there. They were jammed right up against the door. There was nothing I could do; the problem was far beyond my poor capabilities. I am sure that it was all a very positive experience for them: how else could they survive, without swarming together in that manner? They are social insects. But the fact is that there were so many of them, and so crammed in, in one place, that it seemed a little unhealthy, even for them.

So, Lara. Do you have anything to tell me? Come and sit down. By the way, did Madeleine teach you to kick like that? And what, precisely was your relationship with Aurora? And why are you here today?

Oh, dear. For the sake of the girls I am not going to write down what you have just said. It's really not at all suitable.

All right! Wait...! Don't go! If you insist, I'll say it! You are here on a conjugal visit to 'Beaver'. 'Beaver', being a person of great charm and persuasiveness, managed to get the guards to allow you in. He is a man of potent drives, which, if they are not satisfied, will cause him to bend iron and pound concrete to rubble to get what he wants. He must be assuaged, like a rutting stag, even if a few rules need to be ignored. He is friendly on the surface but capable of turning vicious.

All right, now you have made us all blush, let me ask you something. You and Aurora were very close. That being the case, then, tell me – was it Aurora at Larkin's window? Can you shed any light on this matter? And if it wasn't Aurora, who was it? We can eliminate several people, I think. It was not Madeleine. Neither was it Hannah. Nor Guy. Nor Alice. Nor the girl who always said 'Aren't you going to do something?' Nor the girlfriend of 'Dick'.

Larkin usually kept the blinds down at Pearson Park. However, on this occasion, the blind was raised, and the light was on, and it certainly looked like Aurora. A young woman, petite, with short dark hair that curled under her chin. Larkin was in his bedroom at the back of the house, drinking red wine and eating French bread.

I can't tell you how important this is. After all, a man of fifty-nine with a nineteen-year-old girl... It will surely be of some importance for Larkinologists. I lay no claim to being a Larkinologist: I am merely an enthusiastic amateur. So let's have your opinion, Lara: if you are at liberty to talk, I mean. If you really cannot divulge what you know, can you tell us a little more about Aurora – I mean, in general? For example, how could Aurora afford to live at Pearson Park? Where did she get the money? What was going on in that shared house? What did Larkin's mother have to say about it?

Ah, you are silent.

●

I want to say something about the girlfriend of 'Dick'. It is this: she deserved everything she got.

You are probably quite perplexed that I should say this. After all, three people ganged up on her, quite mercilessly, to destroy her... and they succeeded. She was never seen again. But *why* did they destroy her?

The reason is simple. Earlier that year, she and Daniel had been in love. She became pregnant with Daniel's child, and Daniel, for the first time in his adult life, was very happy. He began making immediate plans for marriage: he would leave university and get a job, and support the girlfriend of 'Dick' – not that she had that title at that point – and the baby. He had been looking forward to something like this for as long as he could remember. But without telling him or asking his permission, the girlfriend of 'Dick' obtained a termination of the pregnancy, and went off with 'Dick'. The experience unhinged Daniel for a time, which is why he began to develop his strange theories about reincarnation. He became involved with Alice because she too was a woman with an unusual philosophy of life: viz. she refused to distinguish between people on the basis of their appearance. Daniel began to meditate revenge, and decided to bring Alice in on his plan. 'Dick', Daniel knew, was too spineless to be able to resist Alice's allure; and anyway, in recent weeks there had been some friction between 'Dick' and the girlfriend of 'Dick'. The girlfriend of 'Dick' was still very much in love with 'Dick', but 'Dick' was not perhaps as interested in her as she in him. So Daniel was simply hastening the inevitable. He persuaded Alice to come in with him by telling her the story of what had happened between him and the girlfriend of 'Dick'. Alice was so indignant, and liked Daniel so much, that she agreed to help him. Daniel's plan involved the maximum humiliation for the girlfriend of 'Dick', who, as far as he was concerned, had murdered his child. I hope you are following all this. The plan was for Alice to jettison 'Dick' as soon as she had effected the rupture between him and his girlfriend.

I found this out by reading the noticeboard in the hallway.

I will stop here, though. It's rather dull.

•

Ellie favoured me just now with a rather interesting tale. 'Ellie', I should say, is not her real name: I mean the old woman in the launderette who had cried 'Ellie'. She was in here just now, mopping. This time I am quite hard put to say whether it was a hallucination or whether it was real. The hallucinations are becoming quite convincing. I suppose, looking at it rationally, it must have been a hallucination, since the last time I saw Ellie she was an old woman being loaded into an ambulance, reaching out to me with a withered hand – and that was twenty-eight years ago. She *might* have made a miraculous recovery and taken up employment with the Glasgow police service, but it is not the most likely explanation. Or is it? It sometimes happens that the people we have known as children, and think are very old, are in fact not so old; and when we encounter them in later life we are rather shocked to find them just the same. Take the case of a famous novelist – the same one who saw the dead baby being pulled out of the house – who in middle age decided to return to the little village where he had grown up. This was some twenty-eight years after he had last been there, you understand, and so he was quite prepared to find it had all changed. But the village was much as he had left it: the shops, the school, even the house of his birth, all more or less exactly as he remembered them: they had had a lick of paint, perhaps, but no more than that. He decided to visit the church he had attended as a schoolboy, to see if the vicar was still alive. This vicar he remembered as a grizzled old man, much prone to delivering blood-and-fire sermons from the Book of Kings. So the author drove to the church and parked in the churchyard. It was a beautiful spring day. He was about to go into the porch when he noticed a figure putting up some notices. To his astonishment he recognized the vicar. The vicar hadn't merely stayed the same – he had actually got younger! The author fleetingly felt he was going mad. First the debâcle with the dead baby – it had got into all the papers – and now this! But the explanation was simple. All those years ago, when the author was a child, the vicar had been in his mid-thirties, but had seemed, to the author's childish eyes, an old man; an impression heightened by the fact that the vicar's hair had had some premature streaks of gray. Now, aged sixty, the vicar – obviously a vain fellow – had taken to dying his hair. And here he was, in the prime of life, with a head of thick, jet-black hair. The author was so astonished that he left the churchyard without saying anything and drove all the way home. When he got home he examined his own face for a long time in the bathroom mirror. He even began to address himself as follows: 'You are obviously a fool. You get everything wrong. There's no hope for you.' But then he looked into the bedroom where his young wife was sleeping. She... but this story is going on rather too long, so I will cut it off here.

So it could have been the real Ellie. But, as I say, it isn't very likely. She looked neither older nor younger. This would tend to suggest she was a hallucination. Anyway, her story was quite interesting. I give her words here exactly as she spoke them. 'I was born in 1907 [she began] and came to work in Hull from Hessle, where I was born, when my mother and father died. I was only thirteen. At first I worked in a paper mill, and then took up a job as a cleaner. I have worked as a cleaner ever since. I never married and never had children. Instead I expended all my energy on love affairs. I lost my virginity aged...'

Wait, hold on! Stop! I'm afraid I can't permit that. This diary is for children. There is no place here for smut. And it seems that your life has been nothing but smut. Both in the figurative and the literal senses. No husband, no children... God God! And from a hundred-and-three-year-old woman!

•

There's someone else. The chambermaid's daughter,

Zagira. How strange. I've just remembered your name. Your mother told me that morning all those years ago. What a strange name! Is it Italian? It may be a feminine form of the name 'Zagir'. Perhaps it originates from one of those countries on the Adriatic coast: Croatia or Albania. Perhaps you are only half Italian. How astonishing to remember such a strange name after all these years. Where was that name hiding? In a wardrobe of the mind? Memory certainly does play tricks. Is it because I've stopped taking the pills? I haven't seen you for a quarter of a century and here you are, as large as life. Your clever Italian face, your sparkling brown eyes... You have a very good shape. I really don't care that you must have had many lovers... I am beyond all that now. Please change the sheets on my bed, Zagira. I'll get up while you do it. You are very enticing. Ha ha! But please don't worry, it's just my fun... I'm certainly not going to try anything now, an old man dressed in a blanket, with withered hands, his hair sticking up. That's all in the past. Ah, the way you tuck those corners in! I love to watch people do something they are very practised at. It's relaxing. But of course this isn't the only string to your bow. You have a farm with cork trees, and a swimming pool. Or did you throw it all up for a professional career? Perhaps you became a chemist. Perhaps you carved out a career for yourself in the sciences, struggling for years at the laboratory bench, until finally your researches bore fruit... and the conferences, the admiring young men, in awe of you as you delivered your latest paper, carrying you around the room on their shoulders after the triumphant announcement of your discovery... and later, I imagine, you had to work hard just to keep them off you, had to put up with all sorts of *vitellini* scratching at your hotel door – but you were faithful to your lover, a dreamy-eyed boy, a poet. What did you see in him? Did you love his voice when he whispered to you in the dark? That dreamy-eyed boy who did nothing all day but tap tap tap on his typewriter… he never really worked for a living, but what beauty flowed from his pen! And oh! His blue eyes!

Of course, this is all guesswork. Your mother never told me anything about you except your name. 'Do you know my daughter, Zagira?' she said. 'She cleans your room. She's bored and she never goes out. Would you like to go out with her? Yes? What do you say? You like that, with my daughter? Eh? Eh?'

Ugh, what a dirty old woman! It floored me completely. All my instincts told me that such an offer was to be recoiled, run from… a mother offering her own daughter like that. There is a reason why mothers are mothers, and why daughters are daughters, and that is to stop this sort of thing happening. Though – wasn't it a little like… No, no, I refuse to believe it. I refuse to believe any of it. Ten years to realise she was hiding in the wardrobe, twenty-seven years to remember her name, a hundred years to see into her mother's soul… walking into the room in her underwear… the truth, accumulating bit by bit… disgusting…

Zagira, I hope you forgive me. I hope you don't blame me.

Zagira, Zagira. How I loved you.

Oh, Zagira. There is such a scar on my heart.

•

I now suspect that it was Madeleine herself who was playing the piano. First they treat you to a slap-up lunch, then they throw in a concert. Madeleine had doubtless learned to play the piano at some point in the last quarter-century. Her playing was very proficient. What's more, I am sure she was playing for me.

•

Everyone seems to be here. Lara has still not left for her conjugal visit: it seems she is putting off the inevitable. I wouldn't much like to be in her shoes! She and Zagira are chatting, swapping stories. Ellie continues to mop. Guy and Hannah are gone. And now Alice – here she is, as lovely as ever. She's smoking a cigarette, but it has no smell. Philip Larkin is with her.

At last, here is my opportunity. Come here, Larkin, you old salmon! That's right! Shuffle forward! I've got something to say to you! Who was that girl in the window? Did you not say, in your poem 'Money', that you could have had all the young women you wanted, but that you chose not to? Instead of spending the money on young women, you kept it all in the bank! But what an old-fashioned attitude! Some young women would flay you alive for remarks like that! Guy, for instance! Or Lara! What would Lara make of that attitude!? Better not ask her, she's wearing her heavy boots! What would you have done if you'd seen that notice on the cafeteria door? Would you have acted the way I did, and walked away? Perhaps not. Perhaps you'd have pushed your way through the doors, taken a tray and gone and sat among them, they in their damp woollen clothing, leggings, disarranged hair, rumpled skirts and heavy boots, you in your sober three-piece suit, tie, handkerchief, watch-chain and shining brogues. Would you have affected not to notice their loud talk about women's art? And just got on with your meal?

However – and this is the point, I think – is that poem of yours entirely to be trusted? *Did* the money in fact remain in the bank? *Did* you choose to stay away from young women? I submit that you did not! I submit that after writing that poem you went out and withdrew some of that money. Perhaps the very writing of the poem was a stimulus. You penned the last line and thought: my God, what am I doing? All this time the money's been in the bank and I could have been using it! Thank God I wrote that poem! Now I realise where I've been going wrong! Quick, for God's sake! Every moment is precious!

So I submit, Mr Larkin, that you left your house in Pearson Park and drove to the bank, where you withdrew a sizable amount. You had thousands in there. You had so much – hoarded through all those years of being a librarian – that even the amount you withdrew made hardly a dent in it. You made a large withdrawal – you were deathly worried the bank teller would be suspicious, but she didn't bat an eyelid – and you used it to buy Alice, here.

But wait, I'm getting confused – not Alice, Aurora. Both have the reputation of having had many lovers.

Anyway, not Alice, Aurora. Aurora the beautiful. It was Aurora who was at your window, was it not, Larkin? That unapproachable, ghostly Aurora, that no drag ever brought nearer? What inducement did you offer? How much did she cost? And how did you approach her? Through someone in the English department? Or did you bump into her one day in the street? You were neighbours, after all. Did she exchange condolences with you about the hedgehog you ran over with your lawnmower? Or – and here is a possibility that hadn't occurred to me, I admit – did she approach you? Of course, this is entirely possible. I hadn't thought of it. If so, what did she say? I don't mean in general terms, but her actual words, her *exact* words. I doubt very much if a fifty-nine-year-old man, and a poet to boot, would ever forget the *exact* words addressed to him by a nineteen-year-old girl of extraordinary beauty outside his house, completely unexpectedly. They must be burned on your brain in flaming letters three feet high.

For God's sake, man, get it off your chest! Henry will want to know! If Henry visits me here I can tell him! Don't you owe it to Henry? Henry is of the male sex, after all! He is our brother! Let's unite against these women! Don't let Henry suffer! He's in torment!

So, I will ask you once more, sir: who was that figure groping to the bathroom in the middle of the night?

The end.

A SUDDEN intense light, the light of revelation. The walls... Is this the prison yard? Yes, it must be, and here I am in damp underpants, on my birthday... a rumbling, a roaring, and stones flying through the sky like tissue paper... it's as much as I can do to hang onto my notebook. Strange that it should come now, just at the moment when we were protesting against it. Protesting, railing against it, expecting it every day, every hour... just let me get this down, God... expecting it for a lifetime, an entire globe whimpering in abject terror – those who had the sense – and finally it arrives, at least a quarter of a century too late. I have turned into an old man in damp underpants stumbling amid the wreckage of a once-great city, my mouth and nostrils caked with ash, my ears assailed by the cries of the wounded. To have lived to the year 2010, to be forty-eight! It's obscene! What would Hannah say! Something gnomic, no doubt! Better to have died in 1982, on the alignment of the planets, or on that dusty morning in Winterbank – I can still remember clearly the leaves of the lime trees, and their sticky freshness. Perhaps all the planets are aligned again, twenty-eight years later. Were the last twenty-eight years a mistake? They certainly feel like one! I seem to have done nothing since then but sit around and scribble, and watch television. The Institute? Trash! And the girls? Did they escape? Or are they in the women's block? Was there ever even a women's block? Did they even bother arresting them? After all, what real point would there be? They probably simply let them go. They knew they wouldn't create any trouble – laughing young girls who wouldn't hurt a fly – and so they simply let them go – nothing easier – laughing, merry – and all this time they have been sitting in a bar in Glasgow, guzzling beer. I am sure they have been having enormous fun, hiding from us, with their hair and their radios at full volume... I expect they let 'Beaver' and Tim out too. Madeleine! Why am I still here? I can just imagine what they are getting up to in town. Tim is probably drunk and is explaining, very patiently, to one of the girls, exactly what a lifetime of hard drinking can do to the body. These doctors! And I expect she is rocking with laughter as she listens to him, though perhaps, underneath, she is a little put off by his creased and unshaven face and the sour smell of his leather jacket. Of course this is nothing to what 'Beaver' is doing. We'll draw a veil over that! And so they are all laughing and having fun – though of course they'll have all been killed by now, being rather nearer the epicentre of the explosion. In fact, why is Glasgow not more destroyed? This is not really my idea of a nuclear war. It seems a very small affair. Perhaps this is only the first blast, enough to knock down the walls but not enough to deal the death-blow... the next one will be along any minute. Glasgow would expect to receive at least three or four strikes, seeing as it is situated right on top of Faslane. For now, though, this is really not as bad as I thought it would be. I've had worse upsets. For example, who would have thought that Dr Closer would fall in love with Madeleine? Or Larkin with Aurora? Or Alice with Daniel, 'Garg' and 'Dick'? Or Henry with Aurora? Or the young woman who always said 'Aren't you going to do something' with the young man with the black beard? Who would have thought that we all would have had so many lovers? And so many dead!

I, at least, am still alive and writing this, sitting on a heap of cinders. There is a strange smell in the air that is difficult to define.

Yes – here it is at last. Looking off toward the city I can see the mushroom cloud, brightly lit by internal fires. Behind it, dawn is breaking. What a sight! Internal and infernal fires! Pulsating, evil, magnificent! Growing, expanding with every second, yet sharply defined against the dawn! The end of civilization! The culmination of the human experiment: mass suicide! Astonishing! As astonishing, almost, as the face of Aurora! I wish I had a camera. And I wish Madeleine were here to see it. Not, of course, the current Madeleine, the fat Madeleine, but the real Madeleine, the one who danced with me around the kitchen smelling of mussels.

Oh, farewell, girls! Farewell! You must not read this. I know: I will burn it.

Postscript.

MOST PEOPLE would say that it would be impossible, girls, to remember something very specific – some very telling detail – twenty-eight years after the events. A person surely could not forget something, and then suddenly dredge the memory up a quarter of a century later. They could not recall, for example, that the chambermaid's daughter's name was Zagira, *after twenty-eight years*. But I assure you that it happened. And, in fact, it has just happened again, twice. It must be the effect of stopping the pills. I have just remembered two more things:

The young man whose name I can't remember was called James.

The young woman who always said 'Aren't you going to *do* something?' was called Sarah.

Two very nondescript names.

I have also just realised that all along I knew two *further* things. This time I really did know them, consciously, all the time; but for some reason I didn't let myself commit them to paper.

'Beaver' has that name for no more complicated reason than that his last name is 'Beavor': he is Matthew Beavor.

The young man with the Elvis tattoo is named Kyle. I heard the guard address him as such, I think, at one point.

A strange lucidity courses through me.

•

With very great reluctance I am going to commit to paper the last surviving remark of Sarah, the girl who always said 'Aren't you going to do *something?' I referred to above. I could see no way of incorporating it into the text, since it was rather crude; but I don't mind setting it down here. I feel a strong desire for completion in this matter, since I have trawled through my memory and written down everything I can think of about her, and now there is only one remark that the young woman – who now certainly does not deserve the epithet 'the girl who always said "Aren't you going to do something"', since she said several other things that I can recall – and whose name was Sarah – made, that I have not recorded. Unfortunately the girls can never be allowed to see it: it is a little raw. It is this. It was that evening when I got my shirt soaked, and when I was dancing in that jerky and unskilful manner, and she told me I was beautiful. I think I must have asked her some sort of question about the disco. It must have been something along these lines: 'What on earth do people come here for?' Her answer was this:*

'For love.'

THE END

ABOUT THE AUTHOR

All the Materials for a Midnight Feast is Gary Dexter's first novel. He is the author of numerous acclaimed works of non-fiction, including *Why not Catch-21?*, as well as a parody of Conan Doyle's Sherlock Holmes stories, *The Oxford Despoiler.*